of the *Sultan*

A Master
of the Sultan

Kevin McDermott

POOLBEG

Published 1997 by
Poolbeg Press Ltd,
123 Baldoyle Industrial Estate,
Dublin 13, Ireland

© Kevin McDermott 1997

The moral right of the author has been asserted.

The Publishers gratefully acknowledge the support of The Arts Council.

A catalogue record for this book is available from the British Library.

ISBN 1 85371 706 1

Cover illustration by Finbarr O'Connor
Cover design by Poolbeg Group Services Ltd
Set by Poolbeg Group Services Ltd in Times 12.5/15
Printed and bound in Great Britain by
Cox & Wyman Ltd, Reading, Berks.

A note on the Author

Kevin McDermott was born in Dublin where he lives with his wife and their three children. A poet, he is also the author of several textbooks. He is currently working on his second novel set in Renaissance Italy.

For Sinéad
who wanted a real book

CONTENTS

CHAPTER ONE

Things Bad Begun
Kilkenny 1478–1479

Manus played in the backyard. He sat on his hunkers arranging a pile of pebbles into battle formation. An inquisitive hen came scratching for food. He shooed her away. The bell of St Canice's tolled over the town. Manus paused and looked skywards. He felt hungry, but Máire, the family cook, had told him that he must stay outside until the new baby had come. The little boy pursed his lips. He tried to imagine a new brother or sister. No! he was too hungry. And he felt cross because his father had said so little to him today. And now Dame Alice, whom Máire said was a witch, was in his house. Manus wanted things to be as they had been yesterday, and every other day since he could remember.

Manus felt hot. The sun beat down upon

him. He stood up and made resolutely for the kitchen.

"Máire, Máire, I'm hungry!" he wailed.

There was no reply. An empty kitchen was such a rare occurrence that he forgot he was hungry. He sat at the scrubbed table and examined his surroundings. Without Máire, the kitchen was strange and unfamiliar. The big, black pots frightened him.

Where is everyone? Manus thought. He felt a sob well up inside him. He pushed his chair from the table and ran from the kitchen. He saw Máire hurrying towards him. He ran to her and threw his arms around her waist, burying his head in her wide, black skirt.

"There, there, my little man," she comforted him. "My poor little lamb. What's going to become of you at all? What's to become of us all? Ah no, my poor mistress, my poor, beautiful mistress." And Máire hugged the child tight, hugged him to comfort her own sorrow. And he was startled by the wave of grief which swept over the old woman.

Manus wriggled to disengage himself from Máire's embrace. He felt afraid and confused. Why, he thought again, is everything different and wrong today? Then it came to him what he wanted. He wanted his mother's warmth. He wanted to hug her and breathe her sweet perfume. He broke free of Máire and ran to the stairs, calling for his mother at the top of his voice. It was not an anguished call, for Manus knew his mother would make everything right. That was his mother's power. Máire flustered after the boy, imploring him to be quiet. Manus glanced back and saw her waddling after him. He scampered up the stairs, tired of the old woman's attention.

Outside his mother's room a group of strangers stood whispering together. Among them was Dame Alice. Manus stopped in his tracks. He opened his mouth to call but no sound came. He sat down and covered his face with his hands.

"Mammy, mammy," Manus cried softly. He kicked his feet and his calling turned into uncontrollable sobs of grief. Almost immediately, he was gripped under the arms and lifted from the floor. Without opening his eyes, the child snuggled into his father's shoulder. His father's arms held him tight. His father's hand touched his head. His father's voice soothed him.

"Shh. Shh. Don't cry. It's all right.

Daddy's here." Thomas O'Rourke stood rocking back and forth pouring love over his son. He felt the boy relax and knew he was drifting into sleep. Some minutes later, he carried the sleeping child to a sofa and laid him down. For some moments, Thomas stood and gazed at Manus. "How brave you are, my little son. Lend me your bravery," he whispered, as he turned to face the desolation that this day, this bright summer's day, had brought.

Manus was bewildered in the days and weeks which followed the death of his mother. He spent hours with his father in the bookshop in town. But the door of the shop remained shut, and the sign of the quill and the book was not hung from its metal bracket. Inside, Manus enjoyed the novel confusion created by his father, for Thomas worked incessantly packing books, writing letters, checking files, and the normal order of the shop was thrown into disarray. Thomas's unceasing labour helped him cope with his loss. He wrote to book dealers, collectors and libraries, offering for sale the best part of his fine collection. He did not stop to consider his motives for doing this.

Instinct told him that he could not stay in Kilkenny, for the city was tainted. Kilkenny was the place where Anne, the soul and meaning of his life, had died. Kilkenny was where his daughter's light had flickered briefly, before extinguishing. "No," Thomas repeated to himself, "I cannot stay in this place." Selling his books, closing his workshop, writing to collectors all over Europe occupied him. Thomas feared to stop lest he would lie down and die and he knew that, for Manus's sake, he had to make a new life. But not in Kilkenny. The money from the sale of the books would give him the freedom to travel and buy some time in which he would make decisions about the future.

The disorder of the shop gave Manus a freedom he had never before enjoyed. Books formerly forbidden to him – "No! no! You mustn't touch that. That's not for little hands!" – could now be explored. And Manus took full advantage of the situation. In the matter of books, Manus was his father's son. He did not rush around dipping into books willy-nilly. No. Manus took his time and cast his eye lazily over the sprawl of books. He chose one, an unpromising volume, one might have thought from its lacklustre appearance and, seating himself comfortably, placed it on the reading stand. Manus turned the pages slowly. He examined the letters, for the words were indecipherable to him. In the shape and penstrokes of the letters Manus saw animals and natural features. Here was a curving snake and a gliding swan; and there was the earth and the moon. Manus lingered on an illuminated page. There was a black knight on a white horse. The knight's lance was pointed at a dragon, a sad gold and green creature, not at all fearful. In the background a princess stood serene and unafraid.

"Is she a prisoner of the dragon?" Manus wondered. Squashed against the border of the painting was a small, white castle. People dressed in colourful clothes leaned out its windows, watching the knight attack the dragon. Manus puzzled over the gold disc behind the knight's head. "What is that?" he questioned. He looked again at the dragon. He felt sorry for the beast, who looked weak and vulnerable as the lance tip bore down upon his breast. And Manus felt the delicious sadness of the painting steal over him, and he surrendered himself to it.

Manus chose several other books, and each had its own fascination; but it was a bestiary, an encyclopedia of birds, beasts, snakes and fishes which captured and fired his imagination. The animals were the most wonderful creations the boy had ever seen. He smiled at indolent cats, dozing in the sun; he flew with a winged dragon whose body was that of a powerful lion. Manus turned the pages and gasped with delight at every new pleasure.

"Look, Father," he shouted, at the page of God creating the animals. The golden background shimmered as it caught the light. God, smiling and young, in a dazzling crimson robe, stood in the centre of creation, surrounded by the birds He had made to fill the new world, and the fish He had made to swim the new seas, and the animals He had made to roam the wide earth. And what birds, fishes and animals they were, from the peacock with his tail of eyes, to the pink salmon and the fierce, dark-eyed wolf.

The vibrant colours, the arrangements of the figures and the luminous sheen of the painting wrought its mysterious effect and Manus could not contain his joy.

"Oh, Father, look. Look, Father!" And

Thomas, seeing the rapt look on his young son's face, knew that all the goodness of the world had not died with his wife and daughter. Thomas lifted his child and spun with him, till Manus laughed with dizziness and Thomas laughed too.

For his sixth birthday, Thomas gave his son the precious bestiary and Manus, young as he was, knew the book's worth and treasured it.

When the packing and selling of the books was complete, Thomas and Manus left Kilkenny, never to return. They set out on the long journey to Paris, facing into an uncertain future, escaping from a past that was too forlorn to contemplate, embarking on an adventure that would bring Manus to the greatest cities in the Mediterranean world, though little did he know this as he waved his goodbye to Máire from the back of his father's brown mare, as dark clouds gathered over Kilkenny and the central plains of Ireland.

CHAPTER TWO

New Beginnings
Paris 1480

The first months in France were not easy for Manus. His father was restless, moving from the home of one rich patron to another. Thomas was highly respected and the wealthy paid well for his advice and expertise so money was plentiful, yet his life with Manus was miserable.

Thomas might have considered his son's welfare rather more if Manus had been a complaining, whingeing child, but the little boy did not cry or make a fuss, though he grew pale and listless. One night, during yet another journey in an uncomfortable, primitive, horse-drawn carriage, Manus, wrapped in a blanket, began to whimper and moan like a little cub who had lost its mother, and the pitiful cries told Thomas that he had taken too little notice of his son.

Soon after that night, Thomas moved to Paris and took rooms above the shop of a scribe, in a part of the city where booksellers, scribes and illuminators had their premises. Thomas engaged a teacher, a polite young cleric, to come and give Manus some lessons in French and begin his formal education in mathematics and Latin. A widow, who had rooms in the same building, acted as cook and housekeeper. The rooms were cheerless and bare, and Manus spent most of his time with the scribe, a merry, good-humoured man, who kept up a stream of light-hearted chatter that amused the small boy. And Manus liked the smell and atmosphere of the shop. It reminded him of his home in Kilkenny, and his father's shop in the city. This modicum of stability and security suited the boy, who rediscovered his curiosity and energy and became a firm favourite with the scribe and his customers. Manus, with his gift for friendship, drew his father into contact with people and Thomas's spirits grew lighter and his restlessness eased.

On a Sunday in August, when the heat made the city hot and oppressive, Thomas brought his son to a forest, a great, royal forest that bordered the river Seine, and choosing a shaded spot by the water, father and son set out their picnic. They ate slowly and, when they had finished, they stretched out side by side, lying on their backs. Through the leaves of the trees they spied the lazy clouds drifting past in the immense blue sky. And Thomas told his son a story, for he had the knack of storytelling and a great host of stories at his command. Thomas began, as he often did, by asking Manus a question and the boy, knowing the ritual, answered in the negative. So Thomas answered his own question by commencing his tale.

"And who was this Brendan that the ancient books speak of?"

"I know not, Father."

Thomas smiled at his son and, taking his hand, began.

"Brendan was a learned and holy man. From the first he was marked by greatness, for on the day of his birth the sun shone with a brilliance that dazzled all the men of Erin. Little wonder then that, when this Brendan grew to manhood, he sailed the world over. But one journey was remarkable above all the others." Here Thomas paused. The river flowed gently and the sunlight fell in great shafts through the leafy branches, and in a dreamy voice Thomas resumed. "The journey of which I speak was in search of The Land of Saints, a paradise land that lay west beyond the seas."

Thomas closed his eyes and in a lilting voice spoke the familiar words. He heard his son's breathing deepen and the boy snuggled into him. Within a few minutes Thomas too settled into sleep.

When Manus awoke, the sun had set and he felt cold. He stretched his arms above his head, rubbed his eyes and sat up. His fathered snored in deep contentment as the boy went in search of an oaten biscuit from their provisions bag. He rooted in the bag until he found what he wanted. He munched away and, without meaning to, wandered a little distance from where his father slept.

A movement in the trees caught his attention. Manus stopped dead and peered through the forest. Through the greenery he saw a doe and her fawn nibble at the surrounding leaves. He held his breath for he thought that at any moment the doe would sense his presence and bound away into the deep part of the woods.

Suddenly the doe let out a piercing cry

and tumbled sideways. The fawn bolted in fright but as it sped away it was yanked back, or so it seemed to Manus, and fell over. Then he noticed the arrow stuck in the neck of the doe. Many confusing and conflicting thoughts raced through his mind, but he was unable to do or say anything. Around him the forest came alive with the shouts and movements of the hunters. Four men ran forward and in a flurry of movement the deer were bled and trussed up. As the poachers moved off into the gloom, one man looked around and stared straight into Manus's eyes.

"Look, look," he shouted to his companions, "we have been seen!" Before knowing what had happened, Manus was knocked to the ground and slapped sharply on the cheek. A face was thrust into his. The eyes were cruel and cold. The breath was sour.

"Keep silent, boy, or I will slit your throat. Understand?"

Manus nodded his head and then closed his eyes, not wishing to see the knife held close to his face. The poacher seized him and threw him over his shoulder, moving away from the scene of the crime at great speed, balanced and surefooted. The jolting movements and the sensation of hanging upside down caused Manus to feel ill. His stomach retched and heaved and he was sick over the back of his abductor. The poacher cursed and, grabbing Manus by the scruff of the neck, flung him far into the undergrowth. The shock of being hurled with violent force deadened any sense of pain or hurt Manus might have felt. Fearful of being recaptured, he burrowed his way into a tangle of bushes and young trees. Branches tore and scratched his face and hands, but fear rendered him immune to pain. After some minutes of frantic scurrying, he fell into the hollow left by an oak tree which had keeled over and pulled some of its roots from the earth. There the terrified boy curled up and spent the night in fitful sleep.

It was the sound of wood pigeons cooing in the trees that awoke Manus. A soft light filtered through the branches. He ached all over. His arms and legs were stiff and sore. The scratches on his face and hands stung and smarted. It was some moments before Manus took in his surroundings, but then the memory of last evening flooded in upon him, and he shivered with fright and dread. He thought of his father and rose quickly to his feet, determined to find him. But Manus had to proceed slowly, for finding a way out of his hiding-place was no easy matter, and it was some time before he stumbled on to a forest path. Manus was now lost. He looked for the river but the forest lay all around him. The river. The river where he and his father had picnicked; the river where he had heard the story of Brendan. He remembered everything. In his mind's eye, clear as could be, he saw the doe with an arrow fast in her throat. He felt the breath of the poacher upon his face. The memory frightened him. As he stood in the path, he called for his father in a weak voice, turning in all directions. Even as he called, he knew that it was useless. His father would not hear him. Manus wanted to cry but no tears came. Instead his feet took on a life of their own. They stepped one in front of the other. And so, in a daze with no consciousness of time and no purpose in his mind, he began to walk.

Manus walked without seeing the forest thin and merge into parkland. He walked without seeing in the distance the outline of the city.

A young woman wearing a thin shawl overtook the boy as she hurried to the city's fish market where she worked on a stall. The woman was late for work but she stopped and spoke to Manus in a voice that was kind and gentle. But Manus was beyond hearing and talking. So Marie-Thérèse – for that was the young woman's name – took the dazed boy by the hand and he yielded to her. Marie-Thérèse continued towards the city. At the gates she spoke to the guard, but he took no interest in the boy and thought the young woman a nuisance.

"This brat is not my concern. Bring him back where you found him, or offer him for sale in the market! Be off now, wretch, and let me be about my business." The guard concluded his speech and spat upon the ground, dismissing Marie-Thérèse and her young charge.

Marie-Thérèse moved off slowly, unsure of what to do, but one look at the lost, sad face of the boy, with his staring, blue eyes, was enough to fill her with determination, and she gripped his hand and hurried on. By his size Marie-Thérèse guessed that the boy was six or thereabouts, but he made no reply to her questions. The shock of his abduction by the poachers had robbed him of speech.

Marie-Thérèse knew she could not bring

Manus to the market. As things stood her employer, Monsieur Grenard, would be angry at her tardiness and the sight of a small boy would send his temper soaring. Marie-Thérèse pursed her lips. What was to be done? The sound of a church bell announcing the first Mass of the day gave her an idea. She turned down a street and followed along a great wall. At a doorway she stopped and rang the bell. Within moments, the door opened and a friar addressed her.

"God be with you, my child. What is it you want?" Marie-Thérèse knew from the priest's manner that he would not refuse her plea for assistance. She told the friar her story and asked him to place the boy in a safe refuge. The priest nodded his head and made encouraging sounds as she spoke. When she finished he said, "Father Abbot will take charge of the child. If the boy is not claimed, Father Abbot will make arrangements for his care. Have no fear, my child. You may call to see the child in a week's time, if that is your desire." And taking Manus by the hand, the priest ushered him into the monastery. With a slight nod of his head, the priest finished the interview. As he closed the door, he asked Marie-Thérèse her name and her occupation. Then the door was shut upon her. And Marie-Thérèse felt a sudden loneliness for the boy. Late as she was, she raced back to the city gates and informed the guard where she had placed Manus, lest his parents came seeking him. The guard showed little interest in the information and grinned inanely at her, till Marie-Thérèse left in temper.

Some three days later there was a knock on a cottage door that stood on the edge of the king's forest. The cottage belonged to a fisherman whose task it was to keep a stretch of the river stocked for those members of the Royal Court who wanted to fish, but as fishing was not fashionable with the courtiers, he led a quiet and untroubled life. The knocking at the door caused some confusion, for it was evening and unexpected callers were a rarity. The fisherman opened the door a little and peered out suspiciously.

"Good evening sir," said a gentleman, in a foreign-sounding accent. "Is this the home of Marie-Thérèse Durand, who works in the fish market?"

"Perhaps," said the fisherman, "but what is that to you, Monsieur?"

Thomas, seeing the old man's worried face spoke to reassure him.

"Your daughter, for I presume the young woman is your daughter?" the fisherman nodded, "saved my son's life and I, we, have come to thank her." For the first time the fisherman noticed the boy sitting on the visitor's horse that stood a little back from the cottage.

The fisherman could make no sense of the stranger's remarks, but he felt confident enough of the visitors good intent to call his daughter. Marie-Thérèse appeared in the doorway and saw a smiling face which she did not recognise, and another which she did. She ran forward to Manus and, lifting him down, embraced him with a cry of joy. Father and son accepted the invitation to take supper with the family and spent a cheerful night of stories and laughter with their new friends. And thus it was that Marie-Thérèse Durand came into the lives of Manus and Thomas O'Rourke.

One afternoon, in the early spring of 1481, Manus sat in the shop copying letters on a used sampler, when Thomas returned from Versailles where he had spent the last two days. Thomas was in buoyant mood and spoke eagerly to his son.

"Manus, stop and listen to me. Would you like to go and live in the countryside? We'd have our own house and you could keep a pony and pet fowl. Would you like that?"

"Oh yes, father," the boy replied, catching the excitement in his father's voice.

"Good. You see, a great lord, the Duke of Garrone, has asked me to work for him, to supervise his collection of rare books and acquire new ones for him. He wants me to go and live in the south of the country. And he has an estate house, near his chateau, which he will sell to me. He tells me it has a pretty garden and some acres of meadowland. You would like that, wouldn't you?"

Manus nodded his approval, though he could scarcely take in what his father was proposing.

Thomas continued, though by now he was more thinking out loud than addressing his son, "I will establish a new workshop and unpack my library. Yes, I will stay put, for my heart has settled." Thomas looked at his son and ruffled his hair. "And, my young man, there is a village close by and the children will call and play with you so you will have friends and company. We'll put an end to moving and living here and there. There is one other thing. I am going to ask Marie-Thérèse to come and live with us and look after you. Do you think you could bear that?" Manus jumped forward and gave his father a great, big hug. Thomas laughed. "Right, what are we waiting for? Let us pack!"

CHAPTER THREE

A Divided Heart
Beauzelle 1481–1484

The move to the South of France took place without mishap. The house bought from the Duke of Garrone was situated near the village of Beauzelle, some miles from Toulouse. Marie-Thérèse had never been outside Paris before, but she took readily to her new surroundings. However, she was not prepared for the sudden electrical storms which filled the night sky at regular intervals in that part of the country.

One evening, without warning the wind rose. It whistled through the house and rattled the shutters. And with it came rain, torrential rain, driving against the doors and windows till it seemed the house was under siege from the elements. Marie-Thérèse was nervous. She disliked the dark at the best of times, for she remembered her mother's talk of witches that flew by night to practice their evil upon the poor and the unwary. And the priest in the parish church had spoken of the night as the time of Satan, when all the evil in men's hearts expressed itself under night's protective mantle. And Marie-Thérèse feared the wolves that roamed the countryside, and the rats who scurried hither and thither. She lit candles and kept the kitchen as bright as possible. After supper Thomas joined Manus and Marie-Thérèse in the kitchen, and the conversation turned to ghosts and spirits. Thomas told stories of ghostly apparitions in the family home in Kilkenny and, storyteller that he was, he caused his two listeners to feel a delicious thrill of fear.

Marie-Thérèse passed an uneasy night, tossing and turning in her sleep. At the darkest part of the night, the storm increased in ferocity, and the sky was lit by flashes of lightning that reached close to the earth. The storm woke Marie-Thérèse, and she knew at once that she was not alone. She sat up in her bed and cried out, "Who is there, who is there?" There was no answer but she felt the presence more keenly now. She listened. Outside the wind moaned in the trees and the window shutters shook and banged. The house creaked and groaned. In the quiet of night Marie-Thérèse could hear the floorboards move and settle. Once more the lightning flashed and, for a brief moment, Marie-Thérèse saw a beautiful woman stand at the foot of her bed. Marie-Thérèse screamed and her cry of sheer terror woke both father and son.

Thomas ran to her room and found his young housekeeper in a state of shock and hysteria. She sat in the bed pointing to a spot in the room, shouting, "Go away, go away!"

"But there is nothing there," Thomas reassured her, holding a candle high to light the dark corners of the chamber, and when Manus climbed on to the bed and put his arms around her, Marie-Thérèse allowed the fear to leave her.

"Why don't you sleep with Manus for the rest of the night?" Thomas suggested and the young woman agreed. There was no further disturbance and the household awoke to a fine spring morning that dispelled the gloom of the previous night.

But some nights later, Marie-Thérèse was again troubled by visions of a woman and, when her cries brought Thomas and Manus to her room, it was Manus who spoke.

"Marie-Thérèse, do not be afraid. That is my mama. Can you see her, father? Look, she is there smiling at us. Don't leave, Mama. Mama! Stay a little with us." Then Manus added in a vexed voice, "She never stays long." And Manus stood by Marie-Thérèse's bed and spoke as though nothing out of the ordinary had happened. "Mama visits me every night," he explained, "I told her you were looking after me. She has come to thank you. Isn't she beautiful?" Marie-Thérèse nodded in agreement. She looked to Thomas.

"Can this be true, Monsieur? Is it possible that your wife is here with us?"

Thomas said nothing for some moments, and then he questioned Manus, "Are you sure it is Mama?"

"Of course, Father," Manus replied good-humoredly. "Do you not see her, too?"

"No," Thomas said and there was a sadness in his voice, "but," he continued, brightening, "sometimes I feel she is here, and I think she is happy for us. Come, let us have a midnight feast in honour of our guest." And the three turned Marie-Thérèse's visions into a celebration.

In the days that followed, Marie-Thérèse

asked Manus many questions about his mother, and his answers persuaded her that the spirit world, which she feared, was open to this eight-year-old boy, for he spoke of his mother and her visits to him as he spoke of the village children who came to play in the afternoons.

The house, bought from the Duke of Garrone, was a large, rambling country mansion. It was airy and roomy and Marie-Thérèse filled it with colour and good cheer. She and Manus collected wild flowers from the meadowlands, and Marie-Thérèse cultivated flowers in the garden, so that every sunlit corner of the house was filled with flowers and greenery. Marie-Thérèse had boundless energy. She grew vegetables and kept a splendid herb garden. She filled the yard with chickens and hens, ducks and geese. Like a whirlwind, she sped through the house cleaning, dusting and polishing. Manus spent countless hours in her company. Marie-Thérèse brought him on shopping expeditions to the village, where his Irish-accented French charmed the villagers. Marie-Thérèse enjoyed shopping. She haggled with the miller and the vintner. She made an agreement to supply the butcher with chickens and ducks in return for veal and quail. The village women joked that the pretty girl had bewitched the hard-headed butcher, so favourable were the terms he agreed with Marie-Thérèse, but they were not jealous of her, for they loved her too, loved her for her gaiety and energy and the spirit of freedom she exuded.

Marie-Thérèse kept up an endless stream of conversation with Manus. In her company his French became fluent, though he spoke it in Marie-Thérèse's breezy, colloquial style. Manus entertained her with stories from his books. He told her romantic tales from Italy and Persia. He conjured up images of the Levant and the distant Holy Lands. He related the stories of great travellers: St Brendan, Marco Polo and Noah. He painted pictures for her: Brendan and his ship alongside Jasconius, the friendly whale; Noah's ark on Mount Ararat. In the warm summer evenings they sat by the banks of the river Garrone swopping stories. Both of them agreed that stories about water and oceans were the best of all. They dreamed of cities that floated on the sea and boats that sailed through the air. They shared the same longing to visit Venice where each parish was an island and the roads were made of water.

One evening Manus asked Marie-Thérèse if she loved his father, Thomas, in the same way that she loved him. Marie-Thérèse answered the question in the same grave manner that Manus had used in asking it.

"Your father is a learned and noble man. He is a friend to the most important people in the land. Why, he is even known to the king. And what am I? I am a nobody. I am poor. I have little education. Your father has been kind enough to employ me in his household. And he is a good and generous employer. But he is my employer, so it is not for me to love him, it is for me to serve him."

"But you love me?"

"Yes, my ragamuffin, I love you."

"And my father loves me, doesn't he?"

"Yes, goose, your father loves you."

"So, then, it is simple. I love you and I love my father. You love me and my father loves me. So, now you must love Father and he must love you."

Marie-Thérèse responded by tickling Manus.

"Ah! my little matchmaker. Will you arrange for us to fall in love?" And she jumped to her feet and challenged Manus to race her back to the farmhouse.

But Manus was not so easily diverted. He thought about the matter and realised that his father spent little or no time in Marie-Thérèse's company, and rarely spoke of her. Indeed, Manus suspected that Thomas knew next to nothing about Marie-Thérèse, so he commenced a campaign to bring her to his father's attention.

At dinner Manus made most of the conversation.

"Do you like the flower arrangement on the table, Father? The flowers are from Marie-Thérèse's garden."

"Did you know, Father, that Marie-Thérèse grew the herbs that seasoned our meat?"

"At the vintner's today, Monsieur Thebaud said Marie-Thérèse was the prettiest young woman in the village. Do you think she is pretty, Father?"

"Father, why does Marie-Thérèse not take her meals with us? It must be lonely for her out in the kitchen . . . "

Manus's determination to cause his father to fall in love with Marie-Thérèse amused the former and embarrassed the latter. However, it did bring the young woman to the attention of Thomas and he began to realise the benevolent influence she exerted over their lives. Thomas O'Rourke was an intelligent and thoughtful man. He knew that his household had much to offer the young woman, and he encouraged her to sit in when Manus received instruction in Latin, mathematics, classical literature and church teaching from a local friar. At first, Marie-Thérèse sat embroidering or sewing, taking a passive interest in the lessons, but bit by bit she was drawn into the world of learning and surmise, and her quick, lively mind mastered most of what she heard. Marie-Thérèse observed with great interest the drawing lessons Manus took from an artist retained by the Duke, and she developed her skill sufficiently to sketch the wild flowers that she gathered.

In the evenings, in the warm kitchen, especially when Thomas was away on business for the Duke, Manus helped Marie-Thérèse with her reading and writing. At the end of two years, Marie-Thérèse had acquired the assurance and confidence that comes with education and it was not long before she became a trusted companion in the creation, restoration and copying of books that was to become the main work carried out by Thomas in the workshop he created.

And Thomas abandoned the custom of taking his meals in the dining-room on all but the most formal of occasions, and the three took their evening meal in the cosiness of the kitchen. Spurred by the praise of Thomas, Marie-Thérèse experimented in the preparation, cooking and preserving of food. She discovered within herself a flair for cooking and arranging food, and she nurtured her talent to the point of artistry. Her touch was light and delicate, and her mouthwatering dishes were also a visual feast.

Thomas was proud of Marie-Thérèse and he took to inviting guests to dine with him. When the duke himself came to dine, Marie-Thérèse surpassed herself. She served peacock, stuffed with delicately spiced pork. So lifelike was the bird that, as Marie-Thérèse carried it to the table, it startled one or more of the guests. Even Manus, who knew Marie-Thérèse's ingenuity, was taken aback as the bird breathed fire. This display earned Marie-Thérèse an outburst of applause from the guests and Thomas sat as content as a bridegroom at the wedding feast, as his guests praised the meal and his hospitality.

Later Manus begged Marie-Thérèse to reveal the secret of the bird's fiery breath but, like a good magician, she refused and only relented when Manus sulked and grew bad-tempered.

"Now, my spoilt little boy, here is the secret. Watch. Take one wad of cotton wool. Take one measure of brandy. Soak the wool in the brandy and light it. Oh! see how it flames!"

Life in Beauzelle fell into an easy, comfortable pattern, which soothed Thomas and he lost the last traces of yearning and feverish restlessness which had possessed him at the death of Anne, his wife. For three years, the trio lived in harmony.

In the spring of 1484, when Manus was eleven, great changes were put in train by his father. After much toing and froing, and consultations with the local guilds, Thomas, with the support of the Duke, put an idea into effect which he had turned in his mind for many months. Thomas renovated the stables and made a fine workshop, where he hoped he would create illuminated books for the nobility of Southern France. And Thomas began, again, to deal in rare and precious books. The Duke attached a number of conditions to the development of a workshop at Thomas's home; namely that he, the Duke, would have the first refusal of any manuscript produced by Thomas, and secondly, that Thomas should take an apprentice scribe and a journeyman illuminator into the workshop. Thomas readily agreed to these conditions, feeling the need to bring the world of vellum and parchment and inks and pigments into his life from sunrise to sunset, as it once had been.

The house now became a hive of activity, and while Manus was as excited as his father by the first few weeks of frenzy, the new life brought unforeseen and unwelcome changes for the boy. The journeyman illuminator, one Christoph Le Chou, was a handsome youth who was eager to learn all that Thomas could teach him. Christoph was courteous and charming and had the vision and drive of a true poet. Thomas took an instant shine to him, and together they planned and imagined works of splendid intricacy.

The apprentice scribe was Jean-Luis, a sturdy fourteen-year-old from the village, who was shy and timid and spoke in perfunctory monosyllables. Manus thought him a blockhead, and when Christoph and Jean-Luis joined Manus, Thomas and Marie-Thérèse for dinner – the conditions of employment specified that one meal a day be provided by the employer – Manus lost no opportunity to prove himself better than his father's apprentice.

"Father is going to Paris in spring and I am going to accompany him. Have you ever been to Paris, Jean-Luis?"

"No."

"Then you must come with me, when I go to visit my parents," said Marie-Thérèse, matter-of-factly, and she darted a disapproving look at Manus.

"You will take me?" asked Jean-Luis, not daring to believe this wonderful possibility.

"Of course, and I will teach you to fish on the Seine!"

"So you come from Paris?" Christoph asked Marie-Thérèse, and the conversation ebbed and flowed, though Manus took little further part in it.

Manus fumed in silence for the remainder

of dinner, and when it had concluded, he made a great show of storming from the table and escaping to his room. His behaviour caused a momentary hush but, as he hurried away, Manus heard Marie-Thérèse suppress a laugh, and it felt as if she had stabbed him with one of her kitchen knives.

The weeks following this outburst from Manus were miserable for the young boy. Jean-Luis avoided him, and Christoph addressed him in a polite, distant manner. Even Marie-Thérèse, whom Manus loved with a blind, childish force, was impatient and brusque with him. Thomas said little, but Manus sensed his disapproval and the slight withdrawal of his father's affection was a punishment beyond endurance for a child who had only known unconditional love.

Manus tried to reason things out for himself. He could find little fault in his own behaviour. He wanted to find a scapegoat for his misfortune and settled on Jean-Luis. Alone in the house, while the others worked in the studio, Manus called out names for his father's apprentice.

"Blockhead! Dunce! Country fool!"

But Manus found no satisfaction in this name-calling and felt mean and empty and alone. He went around with a knot in his stomach, a tangle of emotions that he could not unravel. He sulked and was rude and could not help himself. And, for the first time in his life, Manus felt an outsider in his own home. He saw with bitterness that Marie-Thérèse grew more and more fond of the newcomers and he hated them and her for this. So it was a relief to him and to the household when his father announced that Manus would accompany him to the great city of Santiago de Compostela in northern Spain, where the friars wanted his advice on a project to restore some of the oldest manuscripts in their library.

The journey to Compostela was a long and arduous one. For the first part Manus and Thomas travelled in a carriage of the Duke of Garrone. This brought them south to the Pyrenees. To journey through the mountains, they hired a guide and some mules, and formed a convoy with some other travellers. Manus was excited by the prospect of riding high into the mountains, while Thomas worried that they might encounter robbers, though their dress was modest and practical and unlikely to draw attention to them. And so it proved, for the journey was without incident. On the Spanish side of the mountains, Thomas bought two fine horses and they followed the traditional pilgrim route to the city, stopping at the many hospices along the way until, in mounting excitement, they approached the great city of Santiago de Compostela, one of the holiest places in all Christendom, where the remains of St James the Apostle were buried beneath the high altar of the Cathedral.

CHAPTER FOUR

Life is Change
Santiago de Compostela
& Beauzelle 1484–1488

Santiago de Compostela was filled with people who had come for the festival. The square and the streets around the cathedral of St James were thronged with pilgrims, pedlars, and stall-holders. Jugglers juggled. Acrobats twisted and tumbled. Minstrels sang or played guitars or pipes. A harlequin capered and his dog barked. Children ran hither and thither playing tag, screaming and shouting. Innkeepers touted for business:

"Free wine with your meal. Free wine with your meal."

"Fresh fish served here. Bean soup a speciality."

Manus took in everything. His ears rejoiced in the cacophony of sound; his nose smelt the sharp tang of meat beginning to turn. His skin sensed the steam rising from the cooking pots of street vendors. His eyes swept over the stalls selling religious souvenirs: coloured prayer beads; statues of Christ; images and relics of the saint.

The town was joyfully, chaotically *en fete*, and the noise and activity exhilarated Manus. He moved from one stall to another. He tasted roasted chestnuts, cherries and rich fruit cake. He turned this way and that, and Thomas, seeing his son's pure happiness, was unaccustomedly gay and high-spirited. Laughing and joking, the pair took a table outside an inn to watch the carnival. Thomas ordered some hot chicken and bread, wine and water. After the meal, Manus took paper and charcoal from his canvas bag and started to sketch the scenes before him. Father and son sat together until the light faded and they retired to the monastery of St James, in the very heart of the town.

It was in the monastery in Santiago de Compostela that Manus became truly aware of his father's reputation and status in the world of books. In the scriptorium, where monks and laymen worked side by side, questions or disputes relating to the crafts of book-making were referred to Thomas, and his pronouncements were accepted by all as the authoritative judgement on the point at issue. Even Brother Bernard, the most renowned scribe in Northern Spain, bowed to Thomas's knowledge. A young novice, Juan Carlos, told Manus that great care had been taken in preparing for the visit of Thomas O'Rourke whom the monks regarded as one of the most important lay associates of the monastery. When Manus did not respond to Juan, the boy continued: "In years to come I hope to speak French, Italian and English, as your father does, and read the languages of the ancient books, as he does. And I want to be a master bookmaker as he is. For Brother Bernard says that there are many masters of one craft, but your father is master of many." The boy beamed, happy to praise Manus's father and excited and nervous by the confession he had made to Manus, whom he liked, but who was hard to understand and fathom. And when Manus smiled his appreciation Juan Carlos continued, "Your father is a remarkable man. Brother Bernard says Thomas O'Rourke is a man of true genius and humility. And," here Juan Carlos hesitated, "Bernard says that you too will become a famous man like your father."

Manus shifted and felt uneasy. He had never considered his father's work as anything special, nor had he compared his training and learning to that of other boys. He looked at Juan. "Did Brother Bernard truly say these things?" Manus asked in wonder and Juan Carlos laughed.

"Of course," and his smile was so open and honest that Manus did not doubt the truth of the words.

Thomas and Manus slept in the visitors' rooms, but their lives followed the routine of the monastery. They ate in the refectory with the monks. They went to church for vigils, before the sun had risen, and for compline, after the sun had set. Manus loved compline, for in the evening the cloister was illuminated by bowls of floating candles and the monks sang the service by candlelight, their voices rising and falling in unison.

Brother Bernard allowed Juan Carlos to spend most of his time with Manus, for although he was fourteen and three years older than Manus, he was a boy at heart. Manus showed him the sketches he had made of the pilgrims in the cathedral square.

Juan laughed heartily at them for Manus was sharp-eyed and saw many funny, if unflattering, traits in people. One sketch showed a boy gaping at the acrobats with an idiotic expression on his face. Another was a portrait of a man whose ears protruded like the wings of a bat. Juan Carlos took the sketches and showed them to Brother Bernard, who admired the skill and accuracy of the sketches, and praised the young artist. But Bernard was troubled by the hint of cruelty or mockery he saw in Manus's depiction of weakness or imperfection, and he wondered how he might draw the boy's attention to this quality without sounding too moralistic. Thus it was that Bernard sat at his desk in his cell and made a sketch of his own.

When Juan Carlos returned the sketches to Manus, there was an additional one. It showed a sleeping boy, whom Manus recognised as himself, whose head was disproportionately large for his body. In his hand the boy held a pen, shaped like a dagger. The boy's breast was open and from it a winged angel took a small shrivelled heart. A second angel stood by with a new heart. Beneath the sketch was the caption:

Look to Love. Manus flushed when he saw the drawing and took in its meaning. But Juan Carlos chatted on, not sensing his friend's discomfort. Manus thought of Jean-Luis at Beauzelle and felt a pang of regret. And as the two boys made their way to the refectory to help Brother Sebastian, the cook, Manus resolved to make his peace with the household at Beauzelle.

When Manus returned from Compostela, he gave small gifts to each of the household at Beauzelle. To Jean-Luis he gave a penknife for trimming and sharpening his quill pens. To Christoph he gave a selection of brushes, which Manus himself had prepared under the expert eye of Brother Bernard. For Marie-Thérèse, Manus had painted four scenes from the festival of St James. Manus had endeavoured to look with a loving gaze and his paintings were mature and generous beyond any of his previous work.

The gifts caused surprise and delight, and Manus experienced the goodness of giving and understood, at once, that he received more from the gifts than anyone else. For now the demons of misery and jealousy were banished, and Beauzelle was filled with light and laughter, as it had been in the beginning. Thomas, sensing his son's new-found contentment and recognising that Manus was growing up, arranged for his son to commence his formal apprenticeship as an illuminator on his twelfth birthday, in February 1485. The indenture was drawn up and lodged with the Toulouse guild of illuminators. Thomas had overcome the initial distrust of the guild by his open and courteous manner. He gave advice freely and, because his commissions were mainly for those collectors who wished to acquire expensive books which were highly ornamented and illuminated with gold and silver, Thomas took little away from the stock-in-trade of the Toulouse workshops. And the books which Thomas acquired for the library of the Duke of Garrone were so rare and valuable that many important and wealthy collectors came to the area. Thus, Toulouse began to acquire a reputation as an important centre for books. That Thomas was an acquaintance of so many princes and nobles made him a celebrity among the local fraternity of book-makers and sellers.

Manus and Jean-Luis were both required to serve a seven-year apprenticeship, though it would take a shorter time for them to become competent in their respective crafts of illuminator and scribe. And because Thomas believed that a maker of books should know all aspects of the manufacturing process, the boys received a broader education than they would have received had they been apprenticed to a master in a busy, city-centre workshop.

Thomas wanted the boys to be educated, and so Manus continued to receive his instruction and Jean-Luis was now expected to attend lessons with him. In the beginning, Jean-Luis was awed by all that Manus knew and could do, and Manus enjoyed displaying his precociousness. But after some months, the novelty of showing off lessened and Manus helped his friend, and while he shared with Jean-Luis the secrets of books, Jean-Luis supplied Manus with the secrets of the woodland and the riverbank. And the world became a wider place for both boys.

The apprenticeship changed the relationship between Manus and Thomas. Thomas was a kind and gentle man, but he was also a stern and exacting teacher. Manus saw his father excuse the small faults he found in Jean-Luis's work without accepting any minor blemish in the work of his son. Manus thought this unfair and spoke of it to Marie-Thérèse. She explained Thomas's action as an excess of love: "Your father's love for you is as large and unrelenting as his hopes for you as an artist."

Manus did not pretend to understand this adult logic, and he thought his father unfair in this regard. But if this was a cause of irritation to the boy, it was offset by the fact that Thomas treated his son less and less as a child, and Manus enjoyed the challenge of speaking and thinking as an adult. Sometimes Manus tried too hard to be serious and grown-up and Marie-Thérèse often teased him for adopting the tone and manner of an old man.

In the workshop, the two boys shared many tasks. It was they who were responsible for checking the parchment and vellum. Because the books produced in the workshop were rich and lavish, Thomas insisted on the finest parchment, white in colour and smooth and soft to the touch. The boys checked each skin for slight imperfections, small holes or unsightly stains. They had many other tasks to perform: cutting, marking and brushing the parchment. Thomas expected the parchment to be perfect before any work was done upon it, so that full attention could be given to the scribing and illuminating. The boys were encouraged to examine parchments in minute detail. They peered closely at each side, comparing the hair side and the underside, noting how the fibres lay and settled. They learned to recognise those skins which had lost too much of their moisture and those which were too oily. For months, the boys spent a fair portion of their day inspecting, touching and smelling many hundred skins.

Some days Thomas put skins before the boys and told them to pick out every small dot which marked the site of a hair follicle. This was tedious work, hard on the eyes and, to the mind of Manus, not worth the effort, for the dots were almost imperceptible in finished manuscripts. One day Manus voiced his opinion that this work was unnecessary and tedious, but his light-hearted protest was met by a humourless: "You may quit your apprenticeship if you so desire." And, of course, by the time Manus had grown to manhood and become a Master Illuminator, he insisted on the same standards as he had learned in his father's workshop.

Christoph was as much a perfectionist as Thomas, but he was younger and more fun-loving, and he frequently made the boys laugh. It was he who supervised the second stage of their apprenticeship which involved the mixing of ink and some basic colours.

Marie-Thérèse was an interested observer of the demonstrations given by Christoph to the two apprentices. To her, making ink and mixing colour were an extension of cooking. Christoph was a chef, Marie-Thérèse said, who took his ingredients, followed a recipe and created exciting dishes. And there was much truth in her observations, for Christoph mixed fine soot with gum, water and a little vinegar to make the black ink used in the workshop. For brown ink, the ingredients included beer and animal fats. Marie-Thérèse sometimes interrupted the demonstrations to suggest smoother or brisker ways of blending ingredients and Christoph accepted her suggestions in good heart. And Christoph won Marie-Thérèse's admiration for he produced inks which were strong in colour and which ran smoothly from pen to page. After each demonstration the room used for preparing materials resembled a kitchen laboratory, with jars, jugs, bowls, phials, bottles and satchels everywhere in evidence. The clean-up was an occasion of much laughter and banter, though voices were kept low so as not to disturb Thomas where he worked in the writing and illuminating room.

Manus and Jean-Luis were quick to learn and soon they were mixing inks of high quality and making small alterations to the recipes given to them by Christoph. Both boys were conscious of the magic of their art, for were they not transforming a set of ingredients into something quite different from the original elements?

In his mind Manus saw himself as a great magician, controlling and shaping the natural world as he wished. The work with Christoph set off in Manus a train of thought and observations. He began to notice many kinds of transformations: the egg into the chicken; the ingredients into the cake; the clouds into rain; the summer into autumn; acquaintance into friendship; parchment, inks and colours into books of great beauty. His father's oft-repeated saying: "Life is change" began to make sense to him.

And it was during this period that Manus came to regard Jean-Luis as a brother and grew to love him accordingly.

Christoph now introduced the boys to the preparation of colours for illuminating manuscripts. He mixed water with the dye or pigment; then egg-white to bind the mixture; and finally, a preservative (oil of garlic was a common one) to hold the colour. Many of the pigments had to be ground from minerals, a task that Jean-Luis loved to perform. Indeed, Jean-Luis loved every aspect of preparing paint, and he approached each task with a kind of reverence. Manus noted, in particular, the delicate way in which Jean-Luis scraped the dust of ground minerals from the pestle. He noted also how Christoph and Marie-Thérèse fell silent when Jean-Luis worked, caught in the quiet hush of the boy's concentration. And Manus surprised himself by realising with what tender pride he observed his friend.

Christoph brought a lightness of touch to his instruction, especially when Marie-Thérèse was present. He spoke of colours as people.

"Now, my friends, let me introduce you to the Dunce, this brown, earth colour before you. See how muddy and stubborn he is. See, he likes to stick to the brush and how thickly he spreads. You must cajole the Dunce to work for you. Not so my brilliant red. This is Mercury, messenger of the gods. He is swift and light of foot. See how he flows eagerly from the brush and spreads across the surface. He is a true friend. This blue, I call Marie-Thérèse." Here Christoph glanced mischeviously towards Marie-Thérèse, who arched her eyebrows and feigned annoyance. Manus and Jean-Luis threw their eyes to heaven and groaned.

"This Marie-Thérèse is aristocratic," continued Christoph, speaking more for the benefit of the young woman than for his students. "She does not like to be bossed. She is stubborn and refuses to yield. Even when ground to powder, she thinks of herself as glass. See, painting with Marie-Thérèse is like trying to spread tiny crystals of ice. But this Marie-Thérèse is my dearest love." Marie-Thérèse guffawed at this and threw the dusting cloth she held at Christoph. Even the boys, impatient with Christoph's attempts to impress her, laughed as Marie-Thérèse turned on her heels and strode away in a manner befitting the grandest aristocrat.

When not driven to silliness by the presence of Marie-Thérèse, Christoph entertained the boys with stories of his travels. He told them of the time he spent with Fouquet, then an old man, and his assistant, Jean Colombe, the two greatest illuminators, Christoph boasted, in France. And, remembering where he was, he added, "apart, of course, from our own master." With a young man's enthusiasm, Christoph exaggerated the part he had played in illuminating a celebrated Bible for the Duke of Urbino in Italy. But it was Christoph's talk of cities that stirred the imagination of Manus and the boy dreamed of fantastic cities which floated on water or in the air whose buildings, made of gold and silver, flashed and sparkled in the splendour of the dawn. And Manus discovered in himself a wanderlust, a desire to travel to the furthest regions where he would find the inspiration to create the most lavish and intricate books yet imagined.

The work of the studio inspired Marie-Thérèse to conduct experiments in curing and tanning. She sought skins from the butcher which she treated in different ways, in a spirit of scientific curiosity. Marie-Thérèse was careful and methodical in her approach. Each skin was identified by number and its treatment detailed in a notebook which she kept for these investigations. Once she had stabilised the skins, so that there was no danger of them rotting or disintegrating, Marie-Thérèse soaked them in lime, or placed them in pits covered with a mixture of oak bark and dung. By trial and error, Marie-Thérèse produced a number of skins as soft and smooth as the finest parchment used in the workshop. Christoph, who teased and joked with Marie-Thérèse, as a matter of course, was impressed by her skill and ingenuity, though he kept this view to himself. Truth to tell, he was a little in awe of the scientific rigour and acumen that Marie-Thérèse displayed in her enquiries.

But it was her experiments in the creation of colours for illuminating that astounded all the members of the household. Marie-Thérèse crushed, boiled and distilled a variety of flowers, herbs and berries to find new pigments and then blended the chosen colour with assorted fats, oils and egg-white to produce dazzling colours that were smooth and flowing, suitable for application by brush or pen.

Once the colours created by Marie-Thérèse had passed the test of time, they were incorporated in a slow and cautious way by Thomas into the work of the studio. His approval encouraged Marie-Thérèse. Years later, when she and Christoph ran the workshop, she supplied her unusual colours to the stationery shops in Toulouse where they were purchased by scribes and illuminators.

Life in Beauzelle ran its happy course for two years or so until a day in May 1487, when the sun shone from a clear heaven, the river flowed peacefully and the trees wore their new leaves, a letter arrived for Thomas from the Duke of Urbino, requesting him to attend the duke – and who would dare refuse? – at his residence near the great city of Florence.

Years later, when Manus had grown to adulthood and reviewed his life, he singled that innocent May morning as the one which turned his life upside down, a day as momentous as that day, at age five, when he had gone in search of his mother and found instead a host of strangers huddled together in his house with Dame Alice at their centre. That day, the day of his mother's death, was etched vividly in his mind, but when Manus tried to recall the details of that May morning at Beauzelle, he saw nothing. He could remember not one whit of the events of the day. He could not remember that he had gathered flowers for Marie-Thérèse, the wild meadow flowers that she had taught him to love. He did not remember that Jean-Luis, then a big, powerful youth of seventeen, had not eaten with them at midday but had travelled home to see his mother, though Manus knew that it was the pretty assistant in the village bakery who drew Jean-Luis to Beauzelle. He could not recall the smiling face of Christoph who, the previous day, had won from Marie-Thérèse a promise to marry him. Nor did he remember speaking to Jean-Luis that evening of love and beauty and the pain and pleasure it brought to those young and in love. In short, Manus could not remember the ordinariness of a day whose unforeseen consequences brought more change, adventure, tragedy and triumph to his life than Manus, for all his liveliness of imagination, could have imagined.

And in trying to remember that day and the letter from Urbino, Manus did not see the look of excitement on his father's face, for the duke wished to discuss with Thomas a journey that would take him, as the duke's emissary, to the ancient city of Constantinople (which its new rulers now called Istanbul), a round trip of ninety days from Venice, following a route well-known to traders and diplomats, to obtain for the duke's library manuscripts illuminated by the artist Bihzad. Thomas estimated that he would be away for a year. And seeing his son's face fall in surprise and alarm at the prospect of a prolonged separation, Thomas spoke, for the first time, of his intention to send Manus to Toledo to work in the studio of Saul Hirsh, an illuminator and book-maker of the first order. But Manus could not recall, from the vantage point of adulthood, the terror and pleasure which invaded his fourteen-year-old imagination at the prospect of such adventure.

And Manus did not recall his sadness when his father finally set off on his journey. And when, in Toledo, he learned of his father's death, he could not believe it, for had his father not gone away to come back again? And to go away, on one's own volition, was not the same as going away to die. How could it be? But these things were in the future, and the May morning gave no hint of the changes it would bring, save what then seemed the remarkable change of sending Thomas east to Constantinople and Manus west to Toledo.

CHAPTER FIVE

New Worlds
Toledo 1488-1490

*S*hortly after his fifteenth birthday in Spring 1488, Manus arrived safely in Toledo. The city, perched on an outcrop of rock above the river Tagus, was startling. At first Manus missed the lush, green countryside of Southern France. And he missed his "family", as he termed the little community at Beauzelle. Thomas wrote regularly to his son, telling him of his travels and regaling him with funny stories. These letters helped Manus to settle and he wrote back, telling Thomas of life with Saul, and giving an account of the progress of his education. Through these letters and the ones he wrote to Marie-Thérèse, Manus gained a mastery of his homesickness.

Saul Hirsh and his wife, Sarah, were kind people. They liked their new apprentice and

Thomas was an old and trusted friend of Saul, so their interest in Manus was keen and affectionate.

In the beginning, Manus was intimidated by Saul. Saul was loud and histrionic, and Manus could not decide if he was a genius or a buffoon. Saul, on first acquaintance, appeared to treat everything as a joke. The Irish manuscripts, he told Manus, were written in the pot-bellied style.

"See," he said, drawing the attention of Manus to a page of script, "here are the short, round-bellied letters of your countrymen. You Irish eat well and it shows in your writing!"

This was Saul's way. He was a big and jovial man, who liked to eat and drink and tell funny stories. But in the workshop, when he turned his attention to a piece of work, he grew serious and his long, thin fingers moved with speed. Manus was fascinated by Saul's hands. To Manus it was as if the hands did not really belong to his body, but had been added on by some fortuitous mistake. For how, Manus asked himself, could this great giant of a man, with his fat, protruding belly and his wild black hair and beard, have the hands of an angel? Manus watched him bend over a book cover to apply the last piece of gold leaf to the title. When the leaf bedded itself in the adhesive paste, Saul's big, open face beamed with pleasure. He stood back and admired his handiwork.

"Not bad for a pork-hater!" he roared, slapping Manus's arm in jest.

Saul's speech was peppered with similar references to food and cooking.

"Let's cook a book now, young Manus," he would say after breakfast. Manus thought the metaphor apt, for next to books food was the great love in Saul's life. In the early days in Saul's household, Manus worried at the terms of endearment Saul used in speaking to his wife and children: pretty chickens; tasty lambs, mutton chops. Manus half feared for the safety of Sarah and her babes, Benjamin and Ruth. But that was before Manus grew to know Saul's gentleness, and before he grew to love Saul's way of talking.

As in Beauzelle, the workshop store was a cross between an apothecary's shop and a well-stocked kitchen larder. Along one wall were the small quantities of prepared inks in leather pouches. Beside these were kept, in powder form, the minerals from which the inks and paints were made. Jars contained liquid pigments, which in some cases gave off foul smells. Dyes, derived from plants or insect sources, were on a separate shelf, while the precious powder of lapis lazuli was stored in a locked box which was secured to the wall.

On the wall facing the door, Saul stowed the countless brushes, pens and goose quills used in the workshop, as well as the rulers, compasses and templates needed to map out designs and borders. Facing the inks and pigments, deep shelves held the prepared skins. Saul used only the best leather available, the skin of calf, lamb or kid. The hide of young animals made the finest and smoothest parchments. On the floor of the storeroom stood the larger and heavier equipment. Frames for stretching the skins; mortar and pestles for grinding minerals. In dress and appearance, Saul took a childish delight in being disordered and slovenly. However, in the running of his business, Saul was exact and precise. Everything had its place and a large portion of each working day was devoted to cleaning and tidying the workshop.

It did not take Manus too long to understand why Thomas had sent him to work with Saul, for beyond the loud joking was a man of immense talent and vision. And Saul's learning was as prodigious as his girth. Many learned men called on Saul, and they discoursed at length on all kinds of subjects, from Talmudic law to the art of map-making.

One night in late November 1489, over eighteen months after Manus had taken up residence with Saul, there was a sharp knock on the studio door. By now, Manus was accustomed to the number of important people who called upon his master at all hours of the day and night. But years later, when he recalled his time in Toledo, he numbered this night and his meeting with this caller as the most exciting of his young life. Saul motioned to Manus to open the door. Outside stood a man whose driven look and wild eyes put fear into the boy. Instinctively, Manus stepped back into the safety of the workshop.

"Is your master within?" the stranger demanded and, without waiting for a reply, strode purposefully into the room.

Saul looked up.

"Ah, the wild one," he laughed seeing his

visitor. "Fear not, Manus," Saul continued good-humouredly, putting Manus at ease, "this man is a menace to none but himself. He reaches after shadows and pursues dreams, and annoys the great men of our land." Saul rose and embraced the visitor and, speaking more seriously, announced, "But even a Genoese dreamer must take drink and refreshment. Bring some food for our guest and some wine. And then you must fetch the new map from Florence and the Persian manuscript, the one concerning the astrolabe. Am I right, Christopher? This is the purpose of your visit – to peruse my new acquisitions. My, how quickly word travels. So, you want to see what Martellus has made of the reports from Diaz? But that will change little for it is the space westward that fills you with fear and trembling! What say you, Christopher?"

The visitor's face broke into a smile.

"You read me like one of your books, Saul," the visitor replied. And suddenly the man relaxed and Manus saw a handsome, intelligent face.

"Did you know, Manus, that this Christopher Columbus is really a Jew? Yes, he traces his line back to King David. Now,

Christopher, what would your Ferdinand and Isabella say to that, my friend? Or your Portuguese king?"

Columbus laughed.

"I will see you convert to Christianity, Saul, before you will see me admit to being a Jew!"

Saul guffawed and cleared the great oak table in the centre of the workshop in preparation for the map and the manuscript. He told Manus to take Columbus's cloak, and the two men settled down to conversation. And, leaving the workshop to tell Sarah of their visitor, Manus stole a glance at the man whose dream of sailing west to find the riches of the east had often been the subject of conversation between Saul and his acquaintances. To Manus it was as if St Brendan or Noah himself had entered his world, and he fingered the heavy woollen cloak to assure himself of its reality. Manus made haste, for he knew that if he remained quiet and sat unobtrusively, Saul would allow him to stay with the company, and afterwards Saul would seek his views and opinions. Manus felt giddy with excitement and hastened to his tasks.

Manus returned with the map, drawn by

Henricus Martellus in Florence, which included recent discoveries along the African coast. This was the most accurate map of the world to be had in Europe. Columbus leaned over it eagerly when Saul laid it before him. His eyes moved greedily over the parchment but Columbus did not find what he sought. He sighed deeply and pulled back from the table.

"I know all this already," Columbus complained, "but what lies to the west? That is what I must discover." For some moments Columbus sat lost in thought, his head bowed. When he raised his eyes to Saul, he smiled and said, "I will fill in the empty spaces on this map, Saul. I will record what has eluded all others. My enterprise to the Indies will fill men's minds as well as the pockets of kings!"

"Pliny says that west beyond Ireland is an island where all the gifts of the earth can be harvested without sowing or reaping. And St Brendan sailed westward to find a heavenly island. Perhaps you will find the paradise island that the ancient texts speak of." Manus had not intended to blurt out his thoughts and blushed at having done so, but both Columbus and Saul laughed good-naturedly at the boy's enthusiasm.

"Your apprentice is well versed in the ancient authors," Columbus joked.

"Ah, this little one is lion-hearted, Christopher. This is the son of my good friend, Thomas O'Rourke." The Italian guest looked at Manus and bowed to him. Manus returned the bow with all the solemnity that he could command. The two men exchanged smiles.

"Now, Christopher, do you wish to see this treatise on the astrolabe?"

But Columbus waved it away.

"No, Saul. I have read too much already. What I want is to be sailing away. I have lived all my life on ships. It is the knowledge within me that will bring me to the Indies, not the knowledge in books. What I want is to walk in the steps of Marco Polo!"

At this remark, Saul nodded his understanding of his guest's feelings and fell into silence. All three remained lost in their thoughts for some time, before the conversation flowed again.

It was late into the night when Columbus took his leave but Manus could not sleep, for he lived over and over the conversations he had just heard. The tales of a giant race who ate fair-skinned sailors; lands of ice and snow; and places where multicoloured birds spoke the language of humans. And the Indies! The accounts of Marco Polo, who spoke of valleys where diamonds were to be found, guarded by venomous snakes! Manus searched and found his copy of *The Travels of Marco Polo* and, by the uncertain light of a candle, found his favourite passage, and the brightness of the images it contained put to flight the dark shadows of his room:

Within the bounds of this royal park, there are rich and beautiful meadows, watered by many rivulets, where a variety of animals of the deer and goat kind are pastured, to serve as food for the hawks and other birds employed in the chase, whose mews are also in the grounds. The number of these birds is upward of two thousand; and the Grand Khan goes in person, at least once in the week, to inspect them.

Frequently, when he rides about this enclosed forest, he has one or more small leopards carried on horseback, behind their keepers; and when he pleases to give direction for their being slipped, they instantly seize a stag, or goat or fallow deer,

*which he gives to his hawks, and in this
manner he amuses himself.*

*In the centre of these grounds, where there
is a beautiful grove of trees, he has built a
royal pavilion, supported upon a colonnade
of handsome pillars; gilt and varnished.
Round each pillar a dragon entwines his tail.*

Manus paused in his reading. He pictured
the images in his mind's eye, giving colour
and depth to the words on the page. He
pictured the Khan, riding a white stallion. He
placed the Khan, riding from right to left, in
the centre of the picture he was now
composing. Behind him stretched green
meadows, with a river flowing away into the
distance. In a bend of the river, the pavillon
stood with its gold pillars. He saw himself
cutting the gold leaf to size and bedding it in
the gluey paste. He decided to paint the
dragons in brilliant red. At the top of the
painting he would show pale mountains,
bluey-green in colour, growing fainter until
they merged with the blue of the sky. In an
instant, he saw the detail which would fill the
right-hand side of the composition: a clump
of trees with a path running through them; a
grazing sheep unaware of the descending
hawk.

Behind the Khan, on a dun-coloured horse, would ride the keeper, dark-skinned and white-robed. And there – Manus was now sitting upright in his bed – the leopard, wearing a scarlet hood, lying across the horse's back. "Oh yes, oh yes!" Manus cried out, in his excitement.

"I will make this leopard so real that people will fear his power and acclaim his sleekness! I will make his yellow fur bristle and his black spots gleam!"

The leopard was alive now, and moving in the boy's brain. He smelt its cat smell. He felt the breath of its nostrils. His finger stroked the scarlet hood. "Did Marco Polo mention a hood?" Manus mused. "What matter, this leopard is mine now. He is mine!"

And imagining far, distant lands, Manus recalled a poem taught to him by his father:

"Let me tell you tales of my voyages;
Let me tell you the hardships I have endured
Standing on my deck facing the mountainous waves,
Or sailing close to the cliffs.
Oh, you land lovers little know or care you for
The hardships of the sailor!"

And Manus was that sailor as he fell into an ocean of dreams.

As part of his apprenticeship, Manus was obliged to produce two pieces of illuminated work. After the visit of Columbus, and the exciting talk of journeys across the sea, Manus decided on his projects. He would illuminate the passage from *The Travels of Marco Polo* that he loved so much. Naturally, he would use the insular script, the pot-bellied style of his homeland. In his mind he saw the finished text. He saw the strong lines of writing. He saw the shiny black ink. He saw the decorated initial letter of each section. And Manus saw again the illustration he would make. He saw the decorative border around the painting showing scenes from Marco Polo's journey. And he determined that his Khan would have the face of a Genoese explorer.

The second piece of work took shape in the boy's head. He would tell the story of Brendan's voyage. This story would be written in a plain script, with less decorative detail than in his account of the Grand Khan, but the story would be illustrated by the most dazzling miniatures anyone had ever seen, for was he not Manus, son of Thomas O'Rourke? And fired with determination and pride in his father and confidence in his gifts, Manus set to work on his projects, though he was just approaching his seventeenth birthday and had completed only two-thirds of the time required by the guild before he could submit his work.

Manus, in a fervour of enthusiasm, wrote of his plans to Thomas, and was impatient for his father's reply. But no letter came, and when word did arrive it was a curt message informing him that his father, Thomas, had died, caught in a outbreak of plague in a seaport on the Adriatic, *en route* to Constantinople. Manus could not comprehend the meaning of the words before him, and when at last the meaning of the words forced itself upon him, he was overwhelmed by an unassuageable grief.

For two days Manus lay curled up in his room, like a wounded animal. He felt as if he no longer lived in his body. He saw Sarah enter and touch the head of a fair-haired boy, lying still in the furthest corner of the room, but he did not connect what he saw with his own feelings. The food Sarah left for him lay untouched.

On the third morning, Saul entered Manus's room and threw open the shutters. Sunlight flooded the room.

"Come," Saul commanded, and his voice boomed and rebounded from the walls. "You want to learn. I want to teach you. Let your pain be a spur. We will work to honour your father. We will create masterpieces in his memory. Look, Manus. Look. The sun shines. The earth is golden and beautiful. Stir yourself. Come back from the world of dreams and darkness."

Manus sat up and looked to Saul. Saul sat on the bed. In his hand he held a small manuscript.

"Your father gave me this gospel to keep for you. He said I should present it to you when I felt the time was right. This book is rare and beautiful. It is a gift for someone who understands books. It is a gift for an artist. Together, we will take this masterpiece apart and remake it. We will fashion it so that not even the keenest eye or the expert hand will distinguish our work from the original pages. Come, my beloved one."

There was no denying Saul's exhortation. Manus drew himself upright and shuddered. He rid himself of his despair as a snake sheds his skin. He took the manuscript from Saul's hands. Manus turned the pages. He saw the beauty of the book in an instant. He noted too the torn pages; the spots where a pigment had singed the vellum. The feel of the vellum and the weight, the satisfying weight, of the book in his hands soothed Manus's grief. Tears fell. He looked to Saul without speaking. Saul placed his arm around the boy's shoulders and comforted him. Then he guided Manus towards the workshop.

"To complete this task," Saul explained, "we must become the scribe and illuminator who laboured many centuries ago in his little cell. We must find his mind in these pages, discover his preferred methods of proceeding. We must note how he finished the head and tail of each letter. When we hold the stylus, our hands must imitate his movements. We must discover and learn to love the little peculiarities of his pen strokes. We will rise at dawn as he did; we will work in silence as he did; we will pray to God, as he did; we will dream as he did.

"Come, my little lion, let us discover our brother scribe. Let our minds and his mind be as one." Manus looked at Saul and in that moment he knew that Saul would always have his love.

CHAPTER SIX

The Queen of Castile
Toledo 1490

Together, for months, Manus and Saul worked on the restoration of the St John's gospel. They worked with an intensity that brought the two closer together. Writing to Marie-Thérèse, Manus confessed his love for his master, who had taken a father's place in his life. But if Manus loved Saul, he was not blind to the contradictions in his personality. And better than anyone he knew Saul's childishness. Indeed, Manus often mused to himself, there were many Sauls. As an artist, Saul was deliberate, proud and determined. True, he could fly into a rage at careless mistakes, but this anger evaporated as quickly as it rose, and Saul would laugh sheepishly at his own outbursts. Saul the artist could sit for hours at his work. Manus often stopped to observe him. Saul wrinkled his brow in concentration and his breath rose and fell to a regular beat. This Saul, the Saul of the absorbed gaze, was loved and respected by Manus.

But Saul could be foolish and boastful. In company, when Saul drank too much of his favourite wine, he grew garrulous and argumentative. Then he would make wild claims and construct arguments using daft analogies.

This evening, Saul was to entertain patrons and others involved in the creation and sale of books. Manus regarded the evening with apprehension. The guest list included many important personages. In this kind of company, Saul was most likely to act the fool. And so it turned out. Lorenzo Swengli, an important collector and seller of manuscripts, was speaking of a gospel he had acquired from a monastery in Northern England.

"My manuscript is probably the finest example of the insular style to be had on this peninsula," Swengli announced in the pompous tone that Saul often imitated for the amusement of Manus.

"Ha!" scoffed Saul. "I will show you the finest example of the insular style. It is here in this very house. Look," he urged, rushing off to bring the *Gospel of St John* before his guests. "Look what I and Manus here have helped to create. Feast your eyes on this and despair! The greatest manuscript, indeed! Swengli, you sweet-talker, here is the finest example of Irish artistry and it belongs to this old Jew." Saul was flushed with drink and the excitement of defeating his detested rival. Manus was irritated by Saul's lie, for the manuscript did not belong to Saul, but he kept silent. Saul calmed as the various guests examined and praised the manuscript. Swengli looked to find fault, but was forced to give grudging praise to the book and its restoration.

"This is indeed a handsome volume, Saul. Perhaps I can tempt you to part from it. Name your price."

The intensity of Swengli's tone sobered Saul. His awkward glance to Manus signalled his acknowledgement that the book was not his to sell. Saul dismissed Swengli's offer with some bluster.

"Not if Isabella herself stood before me would I part with this treasure," Saul exclaimed in a fit of self-importance. The company laughed, but Manus felt uneasy. Swengli's smile was mean and vindictive.

Manus wished to intervene, to warn Saul.

"Come Saul, be quiet," Manus urged in his mind, but Saul was off again speaking of a journey he had made to Istanbul – Saul did not use the name "Constantinople", as Christians did – and the company grew noisy and merry.

Two weeks after the visit of Swengli and the other guests, the quiet Via Cordoba was disturbed by a commotion and great excitement. Hearing the hustle and bustle, Manus looked quizzically to Saul but, before the latter had time to respond, the door of the workshop burst open and four soldiers rushed in with swords drawn. They searched the studio, as Manus and Saul sat dumbfounded and dazed. When the soldiers had satisfied themselves, the captain of the guard addressed Saul thus:

"Prepare for a royal visitor. Prepare for Isabella, Queen of Castile and Leon, Aragon and Sicily, Toledo, Valencia, Galicia, Mallorca, Seville, Sardinia, Corsica, Murcia, Algarve, Algeciras and Gibraltar; Countess of Barcelona and Duchess of Athens and Ccerdagne."

And Isabella, proud and majestic, swept

into the room. Manus arose and, bowing low, moved from the centre of the room, away from the power of this woman which he felt fill the space of the workshop. Isabella wore a black dress, buttoned to the throat. Embroidered designs, in gold and aquamarine, glimmered like the iridescent eyes of a peacock's tail. The flowing skirt of the dress billowed and Manus wondered if the queen trod the air, for she moved like a divine creature, a being not of the terrestrial kind. In an instant, Manus concluded that Isabella was the most beautiful and the most terrifying woman he had ever seen. Isabella stopped before Saul and stood there silent, stern and unsmiling.

Saul flustered to his feet, wiping his hands in the dirty apron that he wore in the workshop. For a moment he seemed at a loss, and then, recovering his wits, Saul made a deep and dramatic bow.

"Your Royal Highness," Saul sallied forth, in a breathless rush, "your presence in my abode is too great an honour for so humble and undeserving a servant as myself." This outburst was uttered in a whining, insincere tone. Manus blushed for his friend and mentor, and wished Saul wise and sensible, for he recognised that Saul had elected to treat this encounter as a game, and so had begun by aping the manners of Isabella's servile courtiers. But one look at Isabella's face, and Manus dared no more than a brief glance, convinced the apprentice that Saul needed to be real and serious.

"Why," wondered Manus, impatiently, "is it that I can think as a man and Saul insists on acting as a child!"

"Your Majesty," continued Saul, again bowing low, "what is your pleasure? Let me guess. Your Majesty wishes to acquire a precious manuscript for her great library: a Coptic Bible from the land of the Pharaohs; or a book of hours from a French master. No? Then surely you seek a Qur'an from Baghdad, or a collection of courtly poems made in Dante's Italy?"

Saul was beginning to enjoy himself. Manus feared Saul would now give a dissertation on binding and covers, and the deep breath taken by Saul indicated that Saul was preparing for just such a recitation, when Isabella cut him short.

"I have come to acquire one book," the queen stated imperiously, without any trace of humour or lightness, "a book, I am informed, that is beautiful and unique, and which bears testimony to your genius." Saul nodded his appreciation of the queen's compliment. "I understand," Isabella continued, "that you are desirous of offering or selling this manuscript to me." The final remark was made as the queen seated herself on an oak chair which Manus had provided for her.

As the queen concluded her speech, Saul straightened himself and, musing, removed his apron. Gone now was the buffoonery which Saul had put on at the queen's entrance.

Speaking in a grave and dignified manner, which did not quite hide his anxiety, Saul enquired:

"What book do you speak of, Your Majesty?"

"A copy of St John's gospel, executed with a rare artistry, and restored by you to its original perfection. You do know the book of which I speak?"

Saul, his mouth becoming dry, nodded in the affirmative to the queen's question.

"And do you wish, sir, as I have been informed by a loyal subject, to present this book to me?"

For a number of seconds Saul said nothing, and his gaze centred on his feet. He sighed with resignation and, raising his head, he spoke in a hushed tone and with a rare urgency:

"Yes, this book exists and is kept in this house. And it is as wonderful as you, Your Majesty, have been informed. And it has been lovingly restored by an artist as great as the scribe who first created it. That artist stands in this room before you." Here Saul gestured in the direction of Manus, whose heart filled to the brim at the praise given to him by Saul, for he knew Saul spoke from the depths of his being. The queen's head moved slightly in Manus's direction, but she kept her gaze on Saul, and her face was grave and displeased.

"The book was bequeathed to Manus by his father, Thomas O'Rourke. Manus restored it in honour of his father's memory. The gospel is no more my property to sell or give away than the glorious night skies of winter. Your informant, this 'loyal' subject of whom you speak, was no friend to you and almost certainly an enemy to me when he advised you on the availability of this book. Your Majesty is welcome to peruse my collection and choose any manuscript that pleases her as a gift and a token of my good will. But the *Gospel of St John* is not mine to give."

"What trick is played upon me, Saul Hirsh, in this affair? Is the Queen of Castile to be ridiculed and duped? Is this some Jewish foolishness?"

"Your majesty, you were sent here on a fool's errand by those who oppose me. You cannot expect me to ask a young man to hand over his birthright? To do so would dishonour us both." Saul paused but the queen maintained her icy silence. Saul's patience began to wear thin with this woman whom he regarded as stubborn and unreasonable. When he resumed speaking, he was curt.

"I am embarrassed by this affair, and Your Majesty is vexed. With respect, I ask you to remember your loyal (Saul pronounced 'loyal' with a heavy ironic emphasis) informant, who set you on this course. Let him receive your vexed stare."

The queen bristled with indignation. She rose slowly from the chair. As she spoke, Isabella sought to master her anger.

"You are too impertinent for your own good, sir."

"I am too honest, perhaps, Your Majesty, for surely I have committed no offence other than telling you the truth? And may I renew my offer of any volume from my collection which you care to nominate." As Saul repeated his offer, he bowed respectfully, but in vain for Isabella was already turning on her heel. The queen swept out of the workshop and her soldiers followed.

For a moment the air was still. Manus stared at the dust slants illuminated by the sun's rays. He dared not speak. He avoided Saul's eyes. Saul sighed deeply and sat heavily on the chair which Isabella had vacated.

"Bring me some wine, Manus," he commanded, "our enemies strike hard. They hurt us."

Dinner that evening was eaten in a subdued mood. True, the children, Benjamin and Ruth, spoke of this and that, but their habitual exuberance was moderated, and they retired early to their room. When they departed, Manus asked the question which burned in his mind:

"But why? Why would Swengli do this to you, Saul? What reason could he have for disliking you so? Why does he seek to destroy you? This is not the action of a jealous competitor – this is deeper. Why, Saul? Why?" Saul was surprised at the passion in Manus's voice as he spoke and, recognising Manus's hurt, on his behalf, responded calmly. He did not rant and rave. He spoke in jest.

"Perhaps, Manus, because I am fat and he is thin. Perhaps he is jealous of the quail and capon I eat and the rich foods denied him by his physician . . . " Saul laughed at his own jokes, but Manus sat glum and unmoved.

"He fears me, Manus," Saul resumed, speaking quietly in response to his apprentice's mood, "because I am free as he can never be. I fear none and he fears all. And he hates me too, for I am a Jew and he is a Christian who hates Jews. And he resents me for he sees himself as noble-born, while I am the artisan son of a poor rabbi, and yet my wealth exceeds his. And his fear and his hatred and resentment have brewed a potent poison that may yet drive us from Via Cordoba."

Saul was a friend to the Duke of Alba of Toledo, a relative of King Ferdinand and a man of immense power and influence. Alba was Saul's patron and his protector. In law, it was the Duke who owned the house and workshop in Via Cordoba and Saul was employed as a Master Illuminator. Thus, legally, Manus was apprenticed to the Duke for, according to the laws of the Church dating back to 1215, no Jew could employ a Christian. In practice, many leaders ignored these laws, but with the recent waves of anti-Jewish feeling, the Duke had to ensure that his enemies could not label him as a Jew-lover. Ever since the Church had established a council to investigate the sincerity of those Jews who had converted to Christianity and to ensure that Jews were not luring Christians away from their belief in the divinity of Jesus, many Jewish families had become victims of hostile attacks from Christians whom they had formerly regarded as neighbours and friends.

Thus it was no real surprise to Saul when, shortly after the visit of Isabella, an Inquisitor, a Dominican friar, arrived in Via Cordoba to conduct an enquiry into the religious beliefs and practices of the household.

Manus was a silent observer of the interview between the friar and Saul. Saul was polite, but uncharacteristically tense and uneasy. The friar was cold and aggressive.

"May the Lord Jesus Christ be with you," the friar began.

Saul made no more than a slight movement of his head in response. He coughed and ran his hand through his beard and around the back of his neck.

The friar continued, "You are Saul Hirsh, Master Illuminator to the Duke of Alba?" speaking in a mechanical, impersonal way, as if he found it unpleasant to be addressing Saul at all.

"I am."

"You are a Jew?" the friar asked.

"I am."

The friar stared at Saul and spoke with vehemence. "So you refuse to believe that Jesus Christ died for mankind; that on the third day he rose from the dead; that he sits at the right hand of the Father?"

"I have told you, I am a Jew. You know what we believe. We believe that Jesus was a great prophet. We believe in God. We believe that there is a distinction between man and God. The two cannot be one." Saul uttered this statement in a flat, monotonous voice, as if he cared little for what he said.

"Christ is God and your belief is false."

Saul shrugged his shoulders.

"Perhaps, but it is our belief. Please come to the point of your visit."

"The Holy Office of the Inquisition has been informed that you have dealings with converts. We believe that you are attempting to encourage heresy among them, inciting them to practice their Jewish faith in secret, while retaining the privileges open to Christians. We believe that you are a pernicious influence on a young Christian apprentice to the duke. These charges will be investigated. By order of the Holy Office, you are to remain in the city of Toledo until these charges are answered. If the charges are substantiated, you will be brought to trial. If you are found guilty of the charges, your property will be confiscated and your right to practice your craft will be revoked. God be with you."

The friar left. Saul said little. He tidied the workshop and went to Sarah. He told her what had transpired. Sarah came and sat by him. Saul took her hand. For some time they said nothing.

"Will they bring you to trial, Saul?" Sarah asked fearfully.

Saul squeezed her hand in reassurance. He looked into her face and smiled a loving smile.

"No, my sweet, they will not bring me to trial. This visit is a warning. The Holy Office of the Inquisition does not come and announce its intention. Your husband is well-known. He is disliked. He has offended the queen, the devout and pious Isabella. A Jewish upstart has insulted the queen. Someone, perhaps an enemy of the duke, sees in this episode an opportunity to gain some advantage. He thinks, 'Let me embarrass the Duke of Alba by turning the Office of the Holy Inquisition upon his friend, the Jew.' Or a greedy official in the Holy Office thinks, 'Here is a Jew from whom I can squeeze some money.' No, I will not be brought to trial, but my purse will be lightened by a considerable amount because of this visit." Saul paused. He looked to Manus. "And you, my good friend, you must think of yourself. It is not wise to remain here with me. I am a marked man. I do not know how long I will survive in Toledo. You are seventeen now, almost a man. Return to Beauzelle and the property bequeathed to you by your father. I have taught you all I know and you must leave before this trouble begins in earnest." And with forced joviality Saul added, "You are nearly old enough to marry a girl and take her with you!"

Manus did not reply. And then he turned to Sarah. "You and Saul must come with me." Manus hesitated and then, choosing his words carefully, he said, "There is no need for the family to be separated one from the other. I cannot leave you. At Beauzelle there is room for us all. Christoph and Marie-Thérèse will welcome you with open arms."

Sarah rose and, going to Manus, she embraced him.

"Thank you, my son."

"It cannot be so, Manus." Saul spoke and there was no disguising the bitterness in his voice. "France is closed to us. We Jews are not wanted there. No, we must go east. Venice is still open, or perhaps we will sail to Istanbul. The Muslims may welcome us. I don't know." At that moment Benjamin and Ruth came into the room and Saul concluded his musings. "We will see. The future is still forming, so let us be of good cheer."

But after supper, when the children were in bed, Manus sought to understand the intimidation and blackmail practiced against Saul.

"I am a Jew, Manus, that is reason enough."

"But you are many things beside, Saul. You are a linguist. You are a storyteller. You are a Master Illuminator. You are a scribe. You are a friend to many Christians. I don't understand. First Swengli and now this?"

"Manus, you are young and you are good, as your dear father was. But you cannot undo the work of centuries. Our people have been driven from many lands. To ignorant Christians, we are the children of Satan. In their eyes, the plague that killed your father was our doing. The deaths of countless citizens are caused by our poisons. The red ink I use is made from the blood of slaughtered children! Why, Manus, did not my people spit upon your Christ as he struggled with his cross? This is what many believe. Is it any wonder I am hounded?"

"But these things are not true, Saul. I do not believe your people do these things. My father did not believe them. The Duke of Alba knows you as an honest man."

Saul broke in, "But will he go against his church, Manus? Will he go against Ferdinand or his queen? Will he risk their displeasure to defend me? No. A thousand times no. But enough of this, Manus, bring some wine. Let us laugh and be merry."

CHAPTER SEVEN

Death by Burning
Toledo 1490

*B*ut Manus found it difficult to laugh and be merry in the days and weeks that followed. Hostility to Jews spread like a malignant cancer. Those who came to the workshop were stiff and formal, where formerly they had been at ease and talkative. And then there came word that an Edict of the Faith was planned to take place in Toledo, when the faithful would be invited to denounce known heretics. News of this brought a hum of excitement to the city. Hawkers and dealers arrived in great numbers and a carnival atmosphere ensued. The inns were full with the pilgrims who had come from the surrounding countryside. The mood of the city grew more and more excited as rumours spread that the *auto-da-fé*, the public denunciation and punishment of heretics and sinners, on the final night of the Edict, would see a heretic burned at the stake. And Manus was both appalled and fascinated by the prospect; so when the time came he found himself, dressed inconspicuously in a brown hooded cloak, in the midst of the crowd making for the Cathedral square to witness the spectacle.

At one end of the square, on a raised platform, were assembled an impressive array of priests and public officials, dressed in ceremonial robes. With so many people milling round, it was impossible to chose a point from which to observe the proceedings and Manus allowed himself to flow with the movement of bodies. But an eerie hush fell upon the crowd as a procession of priests and soldiers led in the suspected heretics, who were lined at the foot of the platform. At their arrival, the Grand Inquisitor stepped forward and, making the sign of the cross, he led the congregation in prayer. As the voice of the multitude faded, the Inquisitor's words rang out stark and clear. He promised excommunication on those who would hinder or impede the operation of the Holy Office of the Inquisition in pursuit of heretics. The solemn tone of the priest and the dreadful threat of his words stilled the crowd.

As Manus leaned forward towards the stage – and at this time the events resembled to his mind nothing more than a pageant for the edification of the faithful – a notary called the name of the first accused who was brought up on the stage and placed before the spectators. The notary proceeded to read aloud her confession. The accused, a middle-aged woman, stood with her head bowed in such a state of abjection that Manus felt a sickness in his throat. The crowd cheered in derision as her words were read aloud for them. When her confession had been heard, the Inquisitor invited the woman, before God and his people, to acknowledge it to be true. The woman nodded her head, as violent sobs shook her ragged frame. The Inquisitor, in a voice that might have knocked the woman to the ground had not the guards on either side of her seized her arms, implored the woman to repent and save her immortal soul. In a faint voice the woman repeated the denunciation of her sins read to her by the Inquisitor. As Manus beheld the scene it seemed to him that the Inquisitor resembled a giant bird of prey; an eagle, perhaps, full of power and menace. The Inquisitor made the sign of the cross over the woman, and absolved her of her sins. He then called for sackcloth and sentenced her to wear this mark of infamy in public, and before that multitude of jeering, gawking onlookers, the woman was stripped of her clothes and robed in the cloth of shame. The crowd laughed for they were in good spirits and enjoying the spectacle.

And thus the pattern of confession, repentance and sentence was established, and the Inquisitor got through his duties in a remarkable show of power and authority. Like a great magician, he held the attention of the crowd and seemed able to change their mood at will.

Some of the convicted heretics were flogged on the spot. Others had their property confiscated and some were committed to the civil authorities to be placed in jail. These punishments were of little interest to the crowd who were growing impatient, for they had come to see a death by burning, and not fifty paces from the platform, they could see the pyre already prepared and waiting.

Manus, squashed in among so many

others, felt that he was no longer himself but a puppet pushed here and there by an omnipotent puppet-master. For pushed and pulled he was, as the Inquisitor called on the last heretic to be brought before him and the crowd surged forward in a rush of mindless excitement. The last accused was a young woman, a convert to Christianity who was accused of clinging to her old beliefs and of being in league with the devil.

As the guards presented her to the crowd, there was a momentary silence which seemed to settle and linger as though time held its breath. The young woman stood before them, her head uncovered, in a simple brown dress. She was calm and unafraid as if she, and not her accusers, was staging this trial. Her eyes moved over the crowd and Manus lowered his lest she caught and held his gaze, for Manus was overcome with a feeling of desolation and worthlessness, as he stood in the evening air watching and waiting for the death of this lovely young woman.

A breeze blew and it ruffled the gowns of the officials and dignitaries who sat facing the crowd. And then the lull came to an end and the notary read out the name of the heretic, Susanna de Torres.

"Susanna". Manus repeated the name in his mind, and he remembered Saul's story of the virtuous young woman against whom the elders bore false witness, and he wondered whether a Daniel might yet appear to save this Susanna. But no Daniel came and the Inquisitor invited Susanna to acknowledge her heresy. For some time she made no reply and then, in a firm voice she announced, "I deny all the charges you place before me. I am no heretic."

An audible gasp escaped from the crowd. Susanna de Torres closed her eyes and rocked back and forth on her feet. When she opened them, she looked above the heads of the spectators and so fixed and steadfast was her gaze that Manus turned to see what held her attention, but he saw nothing save the dark sky, receding to infinity.

Now Manus was caught in the unfolding drama. He was impatient for the next move to occur and it was the Inquisitor who acted. Dressed in the dark habit of his order, he turned to the congregation and made the sign of the cross over them. People bowed their heads and signed themselves.

"My brethren, we must pray that this poor child be loosed from the binds of Satan.

Almighty and merciful God, do not let this child be blind to the light of the true faith. Let not her heart be hardened against your loving mercy. Free her from iniquity. Cause her to repent."

Manus was shocked by the tenderness of the priest's words. He looked at the face of the Inquisitor. The Dominican's face bore an expression of deep sadness.

"Do you really want to save this girl's soul?" The question escaped Manus's lips and was lost on the evening breeze. Manus looked from the face of the priest to the face of the girl. "No, no," he shook his head, "you are not in league with the devil. Why can't he see that?"

But the Inquisitor was beyond seeing the innocence of the accused. He was binding up his strength to combat the influence of Satan and, when he spoke, his words leapt from his lips with the force of a raging torrent.

"Reject Satan. Reject his ways. Acknowledge your sins. Seek the forgiveness of Our Lord Jesus Christ."

The Inquisitor grew in size before Manus and his strained and taut face compelled Susanna de Torres to submit to the authority of the church. Manus looked upon the

Inquisitor and was afraid. But Susanna de Torres was not afraid and she looked into her accuser's face and laughed. The laughter was quiet and ironic. But it frightened the crowd, who heard in it the mocking jibes of Satan tempting Christ, and the Inquisitor played upon the reaction of the spectators.

"Behold the work of Satan. Behold a heretic!" The crowd muttered and mumbled, ready to express a frenzy of violent opposition to Susanna de Torres, but afraid to do so, fearful of whatever occult powers she possessed. Somewhere the cry rose up, "Burn the witch!" and the cry was taken up and voiced with increasing force and fury.

The Inquisitor spoke to the officials. "I place the heretic in the hands of the secular authorities to punish her as is required by law. In the name of the Father, the Son and the Holy Spirit, amen."

Manus reeled at the vehement note of triumph in the Inquisitor's voice. He felt again the sickness in his throat, and his head felt light and dizzy. For a little time, Manus lost consciousness of what was happening around him. When he recovered his senses, Susanna de Torres was already tied to the stake and a soldier stood by with a burning brand ready to light the pyre.

"Reject Satan and save your soul," the Inquisitor entreated, but Susanna ignored him and stood with her head bent low and her body crumpled, as if the strength had drained from it. The Inquisitor waited and then announced, "I commend the heretic to the justice of Almighty God. May He have mercy upon her soul." He gave the signal to the soldier and walked from the pyre. The soldier leaned forward and set the pyre alight. The fire caught and the flames rose quickly, enveloping the girl.

Manus was overcome by a terror that mastered all his senses. He gasped for air, and threw back his hood straining his neck and head towards the sky. He experienced a choking sensation as if the smoke of the pyre had entered his throat. He thought his tongue was swelling in his mouth. He fought to get away from the pyre. He pushed and shoved, using his arms and shoulders to force an opening, an escape route from the nightmare that was happening before him. People cried, "Easy, easy," and one or two stout citizens pushed hard against him, but Manus was driven by the strength of his panic and people gave way to him. Distinctly, through the commotion, Manus heard the terrified screams of Susanna de Torres, as the flames found their way to her, and in an instant the crowd were shouting and cheering as when a circus performer concludes his act.

Manus broke free of the mob and ran blindly through the streets of Toledo until he tripped and fell. For some time he lay on the ground and great gasps shook his body. He wanted to cry, to empty himself of the horror of the night. He wanted to be a child again. He thought of that day in Kilkenny when he had sought the comfort of his mother's embrace and she was no longer there to hold him. He thought of his father, his quiet, earnest father whose love was steadfast and true. He remembered all those he loved and who loved him: Máire and Marie-Thérèse; Christoph and Jean-Luis; Saul and Sarah. The image of those he loved soothed his hurt mind and he rose to his feet. His body and spirit were sore and tired.

"I do not belong with these people," he said to himself. "I cannot stay here in the midst of this cruelty."

It was dark when Manus returned to Via Cordoba. He slipped quietly into the house and went to his room. He wanted to sleep a sweet restorative sleep. To sleep and forget. To sleep and dream his dreams. But sleep came in fits and starts and it was punctuated by wild, vivid imaginings. He dreamt of flying boats, but the oarsmen wore dark hoods and had blank faces, and in his sleep he heard the haunting cry of a terrified girl and saw the mounting, leaping flames.

CHAPTER EIGHT

Creating a Masterpiece
Toledo 1490–1491

*A*fter the *auto-da-fé*, Manus knew that
Saul and his family, like all Jews and
conversos, would find it difficult to stay in
Toledo. There was too much hate and enmity
against them. And so he determined to
conclude his apprenticeship, before Saul was
forced to quit the city. There were obstacles,
of course. He had not spent seven years in
his apprenticeship, but he believed that he
could produce work of sufficient quality to
overcome the objection of any master of the
craft of illumination.

Saul said nothing to Manus about the
burning of the young woman, at the *auto-da-
fé*. But the death of Susanna de Torres hung
like an albatross around the young man's
neck. Manus felt guilty. He remembered his

presence in the crowd with shame. And Manus felt a vague sense of guilt in relation to Saul and Sarah. He knew that the same forces which condemned heretics in a public square in Toledo would force Saul and Sarah to flee from their home. And there was still a possibility that Saul himself would be dragged before the Office of the Holy Inquisition. Manus wanted to tell Saul that he was not like those Christians who wanted to persecute converted Jews, but he could find no way of expressing the tangled emotions of his heart. And Saul, seeing the boy's confusion, did not try to alleviate it, for Saul wanted Manus to understand the heart-sickness that gripped his people, as the Office of the Holy Inquisition set about its task of persecuting heretics.

For some days, neither Saul nor Manus had the heart to speak to each other, and then, out the blue, Saul embraced Manus and spoke to him.

"You have suffered enough, my young lion. You do not have to carry the guilt of the world on your slender shoulders. Forgive me, I wanted you to hurt. I wanted to see you punished for going to the burning. That was wrong of me, for you are as a son to me.

Your suffering is mine and mine is yours." Saul paused and smiled at Manus. "I am not a holy man, Manus, but last night Sarah read to me from the Book of Micah and I was comforted by the words of the prophet: 'And they shall beat their swords into ploughshares, and their spears into pruning hooks: nations shall not lift up a sword unto nation, neither shall they learn war any more. But they shall sit every man under his vine and under his fig tree; and none shall make them afraid.' Let us cling to this hope."

Manus spoke to Saul of his plans for completing his apprenticeship, begun under the tutelage of his father at Beauzelle, and Saul promised to smooth the way with the guild, if that was necessary.

Manus had already completed preparatory drawings and design sketches for his account of the travels of St Brendan. Now, he gave this task all his attention.

Manus saw this work as a tapestry in which all the threads of his past were woven: The days spent in his father's shop in Kilkenny, discovering the wonders of words and pictures; the experiments in making colours, with Christoph, Jean-Luis and

Marie-Thérèse in the workshop at Beauzelle; the advice given to him by Brother Bernard; the knowledge of his destiny given to him by Juan Carlos; the joy of living shown to him by Saul; his father's gift of stories; his own dream-visits to distant places. All these were present in his work. Manus knew that this little manuscript would express his feelings for all those he loved. And as he worked, Manus felt his soul express itself.

And Manus wrote, in a round, flowing style, the words of his story.

Once, a long time ago, the holy saint, Brendan, sailed westward in search of The Island of Saints, a paradise land that lay over the ocean.

And for this voyage, the saint took with him seventeen of his brother monks.

For forty days and nights, they sailed through the ice-cold water, till the gloom of the endless sea fell upon them.

And as despair took hold of his crew, Brendan called on his God to aid them and behold, before their eyes, an island rose from the waters and Brendan steered his craft and landed safely on its shore.

A great hound stood ready to greet them and he led the monks to a palace where food and wine were set for them to eat and drink and sweet music soothed their spirits.

When they had rested, Brendan ordered the monks back to their craft. Some murmured and grumbled, but Brendan silenced them. 'Do you not know that this is the Land of Sloth? Let us hasten while we have the strength to do so.'

And once more the little craft put to sea. And now they were tossed on the white-fringed waves and wretchedness overtook them. And again Brendan called for deliverance from his God.

And from the heavens a beautiful youth appeared and, smiling, gave them bread and water. And lo! the heavens were filled with a great mass of white cloud from which a white dove descended and landed on the saint's shoulder.

And the dove addressed Brendan in the sweetest human voice: "Sing the praises of Almighty God and keep faith in His goodness." And the monks heard the words of the messenger and filled the air with hymns of praise.

And a flock of birds flew above the boat and they too gave praise to Heaven. And the music of their singing stayed with the monks long after the birds had vanished from the sky.

One bright morning, the monks saw an island ahead. It was barren and treeless, but after countless days of pitching and rolling, the crew longed to stand again on solid ground, no matter how cheerless it appeared.

So they lowered their rowing-boat and landed on the strange island. There they lit a fire and made ready a meal.

But as the fire blazed, and the monks rested their weary limbs, the island shuddered and shook with such force that all were pitched into the sea.

And there they would have perished had not Brendan, who had stayed on board the boat in order that he might pray, rescued them.

And the terrified crew huddled close and watched in disbelief as the island moved away, plunging and thrashing in the water.

At Brendan's word, the monks fell on their knees and prayed. And it came to Brendan in a vision that their island was, in truth, a fish of huge proportions, whose name was Jasconius, and he, in times to come, would be a friend to the seafarers, who wandered the wastes of the ocean as God's servants.

And so their journey continued. Many times the monks were cast down by heart-sorrow, and they thought longingly of their home place. Many times their bodies felt numb, as wind and hail lashed their frail craft. But on each occasion that sorrow seemed their only companion, God sent a sign that lightened their hearts.

Thus it was that the seafarers encountered a floating palace of ice, that glimmered and sparkled in the sun, and their boat was guided through its honeycombed surface by an invisible power.

And why did God favour those wanderers? Because Brendan never wavered in his faith. True, he was afraid when serpents and strange flying beasts attacked his vessel, but he never doubted that God would deliver them and guide them to The Land of Saints.

And after each test of faith, God rewarded his faithful sailor, with a calm sea, or a gentle breeze, or an island covered in fruit-laden trees.

And God gathered the sea-creatures into teeming shoals, and they grazed in the shimmering pastures of the ocean and astounded the monks, who glorified the hidden wonders of creation.

And in dreams, Brendan saw the fate of those who would not answer the Master's call. Brendan saw islands from whose mountains fire and boiling lava spewed upon the wicked. And so terrifying were the screams and cries of the damned that Brendan awoke and celebrated the Eucharist, and he urged his brothers to repent and live lives of goodness and holiness.

After seven years of wandering, Jasconius guided Brendan to the land he was seeking. First the craft entered a great cloud of fog, and as the fog grew thicker and darker, and the monks grew fearful, a brilliant shaft of light lit the way to the golden land.

The island was filled with heavenly music, and on the shore stood the beautiful youth who had appeared to them all those years before. This messenger told Brendan that his name was now blessed among the saints who dwelt in Heaven.

And Brendan drank the springwater of the island and set sail for home.

And for the remainder of his days, Brendan pondered the meaning of all he had seen and heard on the wide and deep oceans of the earth.

Manus was pleased with his penmanship and with the flowing, confident writing of his manuscript. He thought of the movements of his hand, in forming letters, as the movements of a musician making music. When he looked at the pages of writing, Manus saw waves, curving and weaving towards the margins he had carefully measured. Waves of silent music.

And now Manus was ready to paint over the designs that he had marked on the chosen pages of his story. Manus decided to use a restricted set of colours. He wanted his paintings to be dazzling, and so he was lavish in his use of gold and silver. And the colours were exuberant: crimson red, magenta, vermilion, dark blues and greens and purple. Manus was daring. One painting showed Brendan and his monks at prayer. The monks were grouped in three rows of six. The figures, in each row, were almost identical. Manus remembered his father talking of rows of identical patriarchs in the Byzantine mosaics at Ravenna.

"How still and beautiful they were, honouring their God," Thomas had said. So Manus resisted the temptation to make a whirl of shapes and movement. No, he aimed for stillness. He wanted the viewer's eye to be calmed by the monks' calmness, and he wanted the viewer's eye to be delighted by the brilliance of the colours. Saul came and inspected the finished painting. He said nothing. He gazed at the picture for a long time, and nodded his head appreciatively. And then he left Manus to continue.

If the painting of the monks at prayer was still, then Manus's depiction of Jasconius was all movement: the great fish moving against the waves, his tail twisting behind, and the sailors in their craft leaning away from the approaching monster. The colours in this painting were the most subdued of the manuscript, blue, black, ochre and silver, but what a riot of action and shapes and motion!

Manus worked all the hours of the day that he could, and he worked with speed and an unerring accuracy. He felt the excitement of accomplishment course through his veins as his manuscript neared completion, because he knew that he had created a work worthy of his name.

The finished manuscript comprised thirty-two pages. Although, there was no requirement for him to do so, Manus made the binding himself. First he stitched together the sheets of parchment; then he fixed the sheets between boards; and finally he covered the boards in leather. To finish his book, Manus applied a series of geometric designs on the leather. He loved this process. Manus sketched his design, and Saul had it cast in metal and the metal block attached to a wooden handle. The block was heated and then Manus, standing over his book and clasping the handle with both his hands, pushed down and rocked backwards and forwards. He lifted the block and a neat, crisp image was imprinted on the binding. Following his design sketch, Manus stamped an intricate pattern on the leather. His masterpiece was completed.

When the book was ready to be shown to Saul, Manus felt a kind of loneliness. He feared that the effort of making his book had robbed him of all his energy. He feared that he might not find the inspiration to work again in such an intense and concentrated way. And for this reason, Manus hesitated in bringing the manuscript to Saul. To hand it over might be to hand over his creative spirit. Too much of him was caught within the covers of his book.

For a few days Manus moped around,

working indifferently, and saying little to Sarah and Saul. At supper, on the third day, Sarah spoke to him.

"If you have finished your book on St Brendan, I would dearly love to see it, before it is presented to the guild. I am sure you have done a beautiful job. May I see it?" Sarah spoke so softly and with such gentle persuasion that Manus rose, like a child, and brought the manuscript from his room. Sarah cleaned the table before inviting Manus to lay his treasure before them. It was Sarah who turned the pages, and as she did so she murmured repeatedly, "Oh, this is beautiful. This is beautiful!" Saul was silent, but he took in every detail of the work and, when Manus looked to him for comment, he saw that his master's eyes were filled with tears, tears of pleasure at the artistry of his young friend.

"There is little left that I can teach you, Manus. This is a work worthy of the finest master. I congratulate you." And, beaming a smile at Manus, Saul continued, "Let us drink a toast to Master Manus O'Rourke!" and Sarah and Saul raised their glasses in salutation.

The acclaim of Saul and Sarah freed

Manus's spirit, and he set to work on illustrating the passage from *The Travels of Marco Polo*. Manus succeeded in creating on the parchment the image he had long held in his mind, and his leopard was as rich and lifelike as one could imagine, while the Grand Khan was the sum of all majesty.

When the work was completed, Saul brought the manuscripts to the offices of the guild, and Manus had a nervous wait for their decision. He was plagued by worry and self-doubt. He feared that the guild might turn against Saul, and therefore against him. He rehearsed all kinds of objections raised by members of the guild, but the worry and uncertainty was laid to rest when Saul received an invitation to dine with the Duke of Alba, and to bring Manus with him, for the duke had been shown the work of the young Master and wished to honour him.

And so Manus found himself fêted by one of the most powerful men in the kingdom. He made a note to himself to include a description of all the dishes served in his honour in his next letter to Marie-Thérèse. He must tell her that, however fine and sumptuous the food, fire did not burst forth from the mouths of the ducks or the quails as they were brought to the table!

As Manus ate and drank, something worried away in the back of his mind. What was it? And then, with a little laugh, Manus remembered. The date was February 4th 1491. It was his eighteenth birthday.

CHAPTER NINE

Flight
Toledo 1491

The celebrations did not last long in Via Cordoba, for shortly after the banquet held in Manus's honour, Saul was again summoned to meet the Duke of Alba. Under pressure from the royal court of Isabella and Ferdinand, the duke informed Saul that he would have to terminate his employment, and Saul would have to vacate the house and workshop on Via Cordoba. If Saul remained in the city, he would be brought to trial before the Office of the Holy Inquisition. The duke was apologetic, but saw no remedy to the situation other than Saul leaving Toledo.

Though Saul was not surprised by this turn of events and had, in fact, been waiting for this summons for some time, notice to quit Toledo, the city he thought of as home, was almost more than he could bear. Saul went to pieces. He was tearful and angry, by turns. He cursed Swengli; he cursed Isabella; and he cursed the duke. He ranted and raved against Christians and raked over every injustice, real and imagined, that had befallen him in his lifetime. He sought comfort in wine and drank himself to sleep on more than one occasion.

One evening, in April, Manus found Saul in a drunken stupor in the workshop. And, as he gazed down upon the sleeping giant, he felt contempt and disgust rise in him. To see the man he loved above all others abandon his genius and his family hurt the young man beyond reason. There was a hardness in Manus that despised weakness. This was the trait that Brother Bernard had detected in Manus's drawings seven years before in Santiago de Compostela. And now this hardness kicked out at Saul and the words "drunken beast" escaped his lips. Angrily, he left Saul alone to sleep off his misery and his self-pity.

It was in the weeks before Saul and Sarah

left Toledo that Manus grew closer to Sarah. True, he had always loved her, in the way that a son, unconsciously, loves his mother, but now he felt a desire to help Sarah and protect her from Saul's weakness. In short, Manus fell a little in love with Sarah. It was Sarah who took charge of affairs and who insisted on an orderly departure from Toledo. And it was she who forced Saul to apply his mind to the urgent question of finding a new home, a new place to begin their lives.

Saul's bout of drunken self-pity lasted for a couple of weeks and then, one morning, Sarah sat him down and spoke to him, as she often spoke to the children when they had misbehaved. "Saul, enough of this cursing and swearing and drinking. It is time to go to the duke and seek his advice. Is it safe for us to move to another part of the kingdom? Ask him! Will he offer us his protection? Ask him, my husband. Can we join one of his convoys so that we might travel safely? Ask him, Saul. This morning you will make the arrangements to see him. Do not fail us." Sarah did not wait for a reply but hurried away to see to Benjamin and Ruth.

Saul sat for a while, his mind idling on matters of no consequence. Then he sighed deeply and rose to his feet. He ran his hand through his beard. It felt unkempt and unshaven. He realised that his breath stank of sour wine. Saul stood and stretched his limbs. His body ached. He looked around the kitchen. He heard Sarah's words echoing in his mind, "Do not fail us, Saul." "I won't fail you, I promise," Saul announced to no one in particular. And as Saul moved away to wash and ready himself for his visit to the ducal palace, the spring came back into his step, and he put aside the slumber of the last weeks. For Saul had determined on a course of action. No, he would not fail Sarah.

The visit to the Duke was arranged and Saul arrived as sober and wise as he had ever been in his life. The duke met him in his private study and, though the two men were friends, recent events had placed a strain on their friendship; the meeting was businesslike and to the point, and sadder for that.

"Your Excellency, I know you have been my loyal patron for many years, and I understand why I must leave Toledo. Is there any part of the kingdom where I might work in your employment?"

"No, Saul. It is not possible."

"Can you give me letters of introduction to other lords?" The duke shook his head.

"I see. What then, Your Excellency, do you advise me to do?"

The duke said nothing. Then he leaned forward and laid his hand on Saul's arm. The grip was firm. Saul noted the strong hand of his patron, and the jewelled rings he wore. Saul raised his eyes and studied the duke closely. Yes, he had kind eyes, but the mouth was weak. Saul wondered would the duke turn cruel, if he was pressed? He wasn't sure. And Saul felt a sympathy for the duke. He was not a young man, and his high forehead was lined. His face was thin and had a pale, sickly pallor. The duke spoke.

"Saul, you must leave the kingdom and go beyond the seas. There is talk, at this point it is only talk but soon, I fear, it will be more than talk, that all Jews are to be expelled from the kingdom. You know that Granada is lost. The armies of Isabella and Ferdinand will sit outside the city, until the Moors starve to death. Believe me, the King of Granada has no stomach for this war.

Already he negotiates the terms of surrender."

Saul was impatient with the duke's talk. What had this to do with him?

"But why tell me this?"

The duke looked at Saul as one might look at a child who has failed to understand a simple explanation. When he spoke, the duke's tone was vexed.

"Because, when Granada falls, as surely it must, and the Moors are defeated, then Ferdinand and Isabella will rule the greatest Christian state in the known world. And they will expel all those who threaten their Christian kingdom. They will expel all Jews. And when they have expelled you and your fellow Jews, their Majesties will declare themselves the Defenders of the Faith. Now, do you understand? First the Moors and then the Jews."

"I understand," said Saul in a whisper.

"Then make preparations to leave."

"I will."

"Where will you go?"

Saul considered the matter for a moment, and then declared, "I will go to Istanbul, your former Constantinople." Saul pronounced his words with certainty, for this was the plan which had formed in his mind, and the duke's advice made him more resolute to carry it out.

"I see," said the duke, but he was not interested in Saul's plans. He had done all he could for Saul and the matter was over for him. His conscience was clear.

Saul looked to the duke. He saw the older man's disinterest. He knew that he must speak now. He remembered Sarah's words, "Don't fail us." It was Saul who now leaned forward and placed a supplicating hand on the duke's arm.

"I will need your protection to get my family to Cadiz in safety. May I presume on your friendship?"

Saul held the duke's gaze. He saw the duke's eyes return to him. For a moment there was indecision in those eyes, and then Alba smiled, and Saul gave an inward sigh of relief.

"Of course," replied the duke. "I will give you letters of safe passage, and some soldiers to ride with you to the port."

"Thank you," said Saul, "you can do no more for me."

Saul rose and took his leave of the duke.

The succeeding days were busy. Saul and Manus made several visits to the duke's palace. They dealt with the duke's chief steward, for whom they itemised the contents of the house and workshop in Via Cordoba. And it was the steward who made arrangements for the transport of the family's possessions to Cadiz, or that portion of their possessions that Sarah and Saul deemed it prudent to bring with them. And there were some books to be sold, and others to be returned to the duke's collection. The settling of affairs took time, and Saul and Manus spent many days in the palace. And each day that passed brought further tension in the city between Jews and Christians. All Jews were forced to wear yellow badges in public, and the activity of Jewish moneylenders was restricted.

Formerly, Saul's enemies had been few, though they had used subtle craft against him. But now, as he prepared to leave the city, Saul and his family met with a hatred that was crude and unsophisticated. The abuse was mainly verbal and not very intelligent or imaginative. Youths shouted "Christ killers" and "Stinking Jews". Adults spat on the ground as they passed, muttering dark oaths and threats. At first Saul laughed at his tormentors. He mocked their lack of humour. He spoke of their cowardice. But, bit by bit, Saul's mood changed and grew darker. Saul began to fear for Sarah's safety and the safety of their children, Benjamin and Ruth. Rumours of new trials and expulsions reached his ears and he awoke at night dreaming of fires and persecution. Manus saw the change in his friend but could offer little comfort.

The rumours fuelled the desire of many for death and punishment, and attacks on Jews and their families became more common and audacious. And in this climate, Saul feared leaving Sarah and the children in Via Cordoba while he and Manus conducted their affairs with the officers of the duke.

Since Manus had first known him, Saul had often boasted of his sixth sense and Manus knew that Saul had an uncanny knack of predicting events before they happened. Up to this point, Saul's foresight pertained to trivial happenings. Once, when Sarah had mislaid a favourite comb, fashioned from mother-of-pearl, Saul had told her that it would be found on the fourth day. And it was. But now, in the offices of the palace, Saul rose in a minor panic and stood as if straining to hear some distant, faint sound.

"Manus, Manus," Saul pleaded, in alarmed tones, "You must hasten and bring Sarah and Benjamin and Ruth to me here. Quick, there is no time to be lost. They are in danger. Fly, my son!"

Manus did not wait to question Saul further, but made all the speed he could to find Sarah and the children. Hastening through the city, Manus saw a crowd, in ugly mood, move from the shops and homes of one Jew to another. He knew that he must get to Sarah and the children before the mob did. Manus knew too that the crowd were capable of destroying the house and its inhabitants. That thought caused a shock of pain to run through his whole body. He realised that the lives of Sarah and the children depended on his actions. That knowledge caused him to act in ways which were strange to himself. Arriving home, he hastened to his room and seized a set of clothes. He brought them to Sarah and ordered her to dress herself in them. His tone did not brook contradiction. Then he raced to the yard and found the cart used to bring skins from the market. He threw a sheet of burlap into it. He ushered the children into the yard and told them to climb into the cart.

The children knew from Manus's manner that this was not a game. They lay in the cart and made no protest when Manus covered them with the sacking. Manus motioned to Sarah to try the doorway which led into the laneway behind the house. The lane was clear. Manus pushed the cart through the doorway and ran with all his strength.

And then Manus laughed a merry laugh, for he felt light-headed and invincible. The little group followed a circuitous route to the palace, keeping to the lanes and alleyways of the city. And Manus permitted himself a grim smile at the idea of an Irish Christian helping a Jewish family to escape. But the shrill cries of the mob, and a roar of approval at whatever destructive act had been performed, caused him to grip the cart more firmly and run for his life.

The motion of the cart, bumping over the rough terrain, caused the children to feel giddy, and they giggled as they were tossed from side to side. Manus and Sarah exchanged glances and smiled. Whenever someone approached, Manus slowed to a walk and Sarah laid her hand on the sacking to quiet the children. Coming from the market, it was Manus's custom to keep a supply of bones to throw to the stray dogs who were attracted to the smell of the animal pelts. Today the dogs came sniffing and nuzzled the cart and Manus did his best to shoo them away.

As they neared the palace, Manus felt the muscles in his stomach relax, and his vigilance waned.

"Hey, you, stop! You're the apprentice to that fat Jewish pig! What have you got in that cart?"

The words rang out cold and distinct. Manus saw his accuser. He tried to formulate a response, but no words came. Manus panicked and dashed off, pushing the cart before him. Sarah ran by his side. Manus strained his ears to hear the sound of hurrying feet, but he heard only laughter. And then he was struck in the head. The force of the blow pushed him forward and he would have fallen were it not for the weight of the cart in his hands. Manus felt rubbery and insubstantial. He was aware of blood trickling down his neck. He thought of his father, Thomas.

"Please, Father, make them go away. Help me."

Manus shuffled forward, his feet moving in an instinctive way. Manus felt the ground slip away beneath him. The world grew smaller and smaller. The oars of his craft dipped into the aery depths. Gulls circled above his head. Night fell. Darkness came.

The days and nights which followed were a phantasmagoria. Manus drifted between sleeping and waking. He cried out in his sleep. He called for Thomas and Marie-Thérèse. He cried for Jean-Luis. One moment he was in a cart covered by a piece of burlap, the next he was being borne on a canvas stretcher. There were soldiers mounted on horseback. Through a window he saw their breastplates gleam in the sun. Figures from his books and from his life roamed in and out of his head. Marco Polo and Christopher Columbus waved to him from a three-masted ship, as it sailed into the Mediterranean from the port of Cadiz. And then, one bright morning, in August 1491, Manus came to his senses. He lay in a narrow bed, in surroundings that were not familiar. He stayed still and listened. What was that sound? He tried to place it. And then it came to him. It was the sea. The sea lapping the sides of a ship. And then Manus felt the motion of the waves. He was at sea. He was Brendan the Navigator; he was Marco Polo; he was Father Noah; he was every sailor who had ever put to sea. He was the seafarer of his father's poem. Manus O'Rourke, seafarer.

CHAPTER TEN

The Levant
Istanbul 1491–1492

Ruth and Benjamin were the first to discover that Manus had come back to life. They hugged and kissed him and spoke in a whirl of excitement, in answer to his questions.

"Am I on a ship?"

"Yes," they told him. "We are on a ship. A Moorish ship bound for Istanbul."

"Istanbul!" Manus sat up as if to jump from his bed. The sudden movement brought a dart of pain that affected his entire body. Dizzy and weak, he lay still. Gingerly, he felt his head. "What happened to me?"

"Don't you remember?" Ruth asked.

"No, I don't."

"You were struck on the head by a rock and collapsed but Mother bundled you into the cart where we were hiding. We jumped out," here Ruth spoke with self-conscious pride, "and we helped to push you to the safety of the Duke of Alba's palace."

There was a pause as memory stirred in Manus. "I recollect the cart." He reached out his hand and took hers in his. "Thank you."

Ruth blushed and lowered her eyes. Benjamin broke in.

"Manus, you missed all the excitement. The duke gave us a mounted escort and two carriages. We rode like the wind south to Cadiz."

Ruth looked into Manus's pale face. "And Mother thought the bumping and rolling of the carriage would kill you." Benjamin made a dismissive grunt.

"But we didn't slow down, for Father said we had to make all possible speed. And we rode for four days, stopping only to change horses."

The children talked incessantly, interrupting and contradicting each other.

"At the port, Father sought out a Moorish captain and paid him to take us."

"No, he didn't pay him. The ship had representatives of the King of Granada on board and they knew of Father and invited him aboard as their guest. So we sail upon a royal ship!"

"Father paid."

"He didn't. You know nothing, Benjamin."

Tears were threatening so Manus broke in. "How long have we been at sea?"

Ruth considered for a moment. "A week. Already we have landed at Algiers. All the nations of the world were there, Manus! Armenians, Greeks, Genoese, Turks, Moors and Jews. We watched from the deck as the fresh water and supplies were loaded. Father greeted a Jew in Hebrew and the two conversed. The day after tomorrow we will dock at Tunis!"

"Tunis?" Manus repeated incredulously. "Then we are really on our way to Istanbul! This is like a dream."

When Saul and Sarah heard of Manus's recovery they rushed to greet him. At once Manus saw that Saul was ebullient with the excitement of new beginnings. He had gathered all his optimism to himself. The past was behind.

Manus made a speedy recovery. The journey in the light caravel was not difficult. The ship hugged the land along the North African coastline, and the weather in August was still. The dry air, warmed by the desert breezes, the clear light and the vastness of the blue sky above the Mediterranean acted as restoratives. Manus spent most of his time on deck, sketching and writing. The landscape he saw as they sailed into Tunis was no different from the rocky terrain around Toledo. Here, as there, farmers moved across the face of the earth. There were orange groves and vineyards. Only the palm trees told him that he had left Spain behind. And the realisation came to Manus that the world, from east to west and from north to south, was really one world. Men and women strove in the same way to dominate the earth and the weather. And yet men's hearts were divided. The Moors, upon whose ship he sailed, and Saul's family, whom he loved, were not wanted in Christian Spain. Manus shook his head in sadness. Yet, truth to tell, it was hard to be sad amid the beauty of the Mediterranean.

In the port of Tunis, Manus watched the ships load and unload. There was incessant movement and carrying. Sacks of almonds from Marseilles. Spices from the East. Silk, carried from China to Istanbul along the great caravan routes, and now on the final leg of its journey to the capitals of Europe. There were crates of oranges, lemons and pomegranates. Giant tunny fish lay waiting to be salted. Cargoes of wax, wool and leather stood on the quayside ready for dispatch. Yes, thought Manus, the goods of the world move in circles!

His ship was not taking on cargo. The aim of the Moors was to get to Istanbul as quickly as possible, in order to petition the Sultan to intercede in the war against the Spanish monarchs. As soon as water and fresh food was taken on board, the craft set out to traverse the wide expanse of ocean that separated the coast of Africa from the island of Sicily.

Now, for the first time since leaving Cadiz, the ship had to negotiate an angry and unsettled sea. Manus was not unnerved as the ship rose and fell, though Sarah and the children took to their tiny compartment below the afterdeck. He waited eagerly to catch his first sight of Sicily, the land of the Greeks. In these waters Odysseus had piloted his vessel between Scylla and Charbydis. Now Manus followed in his footsteps. Under a glorious sky, they sailed through the fearful channel on a sea that was calm and gentle. There was no whirlpool and no monster. So Manus sketched a likeness of the dreaded Scylla. A sea-serpent, with six heads and a girdle of snarling dogs. He didn't want to make her ugly, for she had been loved by Poseidon and it was through the jealousy of the god's wife that she had acquired her monstrous form. So he drew a beautiful face, sad and bitter. The same face repeated six times. The face of love turned sour. Manus was pleased with his sketch and decided to send it to Marie-Thérèse, when he wrote to her and Christoph with a description of his voyage.

As they cleared the channel and hugged the Italian coast, Manus looked back to Sicily. Faintly, through the haze, he saw Mount Etna like an island floating on a sea of clouds.

Soon, there was more open sea to be crossed as the voyagers made for Corfu. The town was a Venetian port and the ship was obliged to pay heavy taxes for a berth. The emissaries from Granada elected to spend one night on *terra firma*. So Saul and his family, with Manus in tow, disembarked.

After two weeks on the sea, the earth felt strange. The Jewish community on the island welcomed Saul and he told them of developments in Spain. As his master spoke, Manus saw the unease in the faces of the listeners. More than most, they understood uncertainty. Did they not live under the protection of a Christian empire that was far from their shores, while on their doorstep the covetous Turks looked down upon them from the mountains on the mainland, separated by no more than three miles of water? Those dark mountains troubled the loyal subjects of the Venetian Republic.

Next morning the ship set off again on the final leg of its journey, making for Modon, where they would swing round eastward to find the Aegean Sea. Here, Manus knew, the ancient world was still alive. And he knew, too, that he would bring the landscape and the blue of these skies into the pages of future manuscripts. In his mind he saw the fall of Icarus and Theseus's ship making for Athens with its black sail catching the wind.

Across these waters, at the journey's end, lay the Bosporus, gateway to the Black Sea, whose furthest shores were barren wastelands. To those distant lands Ovid had been banished for offending the Roman emperor; an exile that was a kind of death to the poet. Yet, to Manus, the Bosporus was the gateway to life and adventure.

At the end of a month of voyaging, the ship sailed into a crimson and gold sun that hung low over the city. Behind them the moon was already high in the sky. Manus could scarcely contain his excitement. When the city, in its evening splendour, came into full view, Manus gripped the handrail and fought back the tears that welled inside him. Saul stood in the prow of the ship, large and laughing, like the personification of wind or some other elemental force. And, turning to his young friend, he cried out, "Behold the city of all cities. Behold the city of dreams. Behold Byzantium! Behold Constantinople! Behold Istanbul!"

February 1492.

Dear Marie-Thérèse and Christoph,
   Today is my nineteenth birthday. And my thoughts are with you. How long is it since I have seen you all and our lovely

house in Beauzelle? Too long. Some days I yearn to be back working alongside you both, creating beautiful books together!

So much has happened to me in the last months. Where should I begin? Today, perhaps. Yes, today I sit here, in this garden of tranquillity, writing to you. I sit in the garden of the Sultan Beyazid, who is called the Pious by his people.

And he is indeed holy and pious. The Sultan has welcomed us with open arms. He knew of Saul, for some years ago Saul restored a Qur'an which the King of Granada presented to him. The Sultan loves calligraphy above all the other arts and he holds Saul in such high regard that he holds the inkwell when Saul works! I joke not. I have seen the Sultan, with my own eyes, hold the inkwell while Saul wrote on the parchment!

There is so much to tell you. My mind is in a jumble. Did I say that we are in the Sultan's employment? Yes. I work for the Sultan Beyazid, in the workshops of the palace. And what workshops and artists there are here! There are ten illuminators, and the same number of scribes. And there are weavers, potters and enamellers. We are a city of artisans. But we are a community. There is no jealousy among us, or at least not of the kind we found in Toledo. No. The Turks accept us. The Sultan speaks Italian and some Spanish and we are learning to speak the language of the Turks. I am quite the scholar, for Saul teaches me the Arab script. And I have never been happier in my life, though, of course, I miss you all.

Do not be alarmed for me, dear friends. The sadness and disappointment of our flight from Toledo is long past. Forgive me if my letters to you were full of doubt and uncertainty. All is changed now for the better. Do you remember, Marie-Thérèse, when we first moved to Beauzelle, my mother appeared to you? Well, in the nights on board ship, before we reached Istanbul, she was present in my dreams. It is ten years, I am sure, since she came to me. But she was with me on my journey and how she comforted my spirits!

Marie-Thérèse, I feel that I am walking in my father's footsteps. The Duke of Urbino wrote to the Sultan telling him that my father would come on his behalf. He never arrived, but I am here now, in his stead.

And the work we do! It is a matter of pride to the Sultan that his gifts to visiting ambassadors are of the most lavish and ornate kind. So, Saul and I work on those manuscripts which are to be written in French or Italian or English. And the Sultan likes to present each ambassador with a scroll containing a wise saying of the Prophet Mohammed. Sometimes, we work on the scrolls too. You should hear Saul laugh and joke about his new religion!

In Istanbul, Saul is a new man. For a time, I thought I would grow to hate him, for he was full of self-pity and wasteful despair, but the Levant has revitalised him. He produces work that is truly beautiful. And his soul is calm. I think you would admire his work, Christoph, and you might even appreciate his jokes!

The Sultan speaks to Saul on many subjects, and Saul has won his confidence. Saul has heard that soon Isabella and Ferdinand will issue a decree expelling all Jews from their territory. Therefore, Saul has asked the Sultan to open his heart and his kingdom to the Jews. I overheard Saul speak thus to Beyazid:

"Think, Your Highness, of all those doctors, mathematicians, astronomers and merchants. Think what benefit your kingdom would derive from their presence." And the Sultan responded by saying that all humanity was welcome to his land. Buoyed by this, Saul has discussed plans with an admiral of the fleet for sending a flotilla of ships to bring the Jews to this paradise land. Maybe, at the end of all, I have landed on the island that Brendan found long ago! Certainly, I have voyaged far as he did. I wonder will I ever go back to Ireland? I think not for I remember so little of it.

Often I think of Jean-Luis. He must write to me! The girls here are beautiful, and I believe I am a little in love with one of the nieces of the Sultan! How I wish Jean-Luis could advise me! But perhaps he is too old to think about such matters as love! And you too must write with all the news of the workshop.

But truly I am happy here, and have been from the moment we landed. I will never forget arriving in the city. The quayside was *thronged with people and camels. And I saw a little boy hold a monkey on a leash. What colour and excitement! It brought back to me my visit to Santiago de Compostela with Father, many years ago. And the excitement has not left my heart.*

So, my friends, you see I am happy. Yes. I am happy and my heart is free. My heart is free.

CHAPTER ELEVEN

A Master of the Sultan
Istanbul 1495

Manus stood on the quayside as the ship began its journey westward to Venice. The golden orb of the sun hung low in the sky, burnishing the waters of the Bosporus. Manus waited until the figures waving to him from the deck were no more than specks on the horizon. Then he turned for home. Manus smiled to himself. "Home". Yes, he was going home. Three years after arriving in Istanbul, Saul was retracing some of his steps. At the request of the Sultan, he was going to Venice as ambassador of the Ottoman empire. There were risks, perhaps, in returning to Europe, but in Venice there were many Jews living in the city and there were Jewish communities in every part of the empire. The Venetian Republic did not bow to the wishes of Rome, least of all in matters concerning the suppression of Jews. No, Saul would be safe in Venice. Indeed, as representative of the Sultan, he would be an honoured personage. The source of Venice's wealth lay in its trade with the East. The continuance and development of that trade dictated that every opportunity be taken to foster good relations between the Republic and the Sultan.

Manus had never seen Venice, but in his mind's eye he pictured the arrival of Saul in the city from all he had been told of it. The banners in red silk with the golden figure of the winged lion, the symbol of the evangelist Mark, fluttering in the breeze. The sultan's ship anchored in the basin before St Mark's Square. Saul and his retinue being carried to the Doge's palace in gondolas. The members of the senate and the grand council with the Doge himself, splendid in his jewelled hat woven of gold and silver, waiting to greet them. Saul stepping ashore under the granite columns that marked the gateway to the city, watched over by St Theodore slaying a dragon and the bronze, winged lion. Manus saw it all and saw Saul's boyish pleasure in everything.

Part of Manus wanted to be there to see

the spectacle and, later, to walk the streets of Venice. But he could not face journeying westward. The cries of Susanna de Torres still rang in his ears. He needed to be as far away from them as he could be. And, now that Saul was gone, he would take over the preparation of all manuscripts in the western style for the Sultan. Tomorrow he would be summoned by Beyazid and presented with a golden inkwell and pen. He would become Master Illuminator in the court of the Sultan. The thought of that honour filled Manus with a sense of pride and pleasure.

Making his way from the quayside, Manus took in the sights and sounds of the city. The smell of fish being fried. The stalls of spices under miles of white canopy. The fruit sellers. That he was in love with the Sultan's niece and intended to marry her encouraged the generous way he looked upon the world. He was twenty-two years of age, and the future lay before him like a bright, shimmering stream. And tomorrow the Sultan would summon him.

But this morning there was no hurry. Manus made for the Grand Bazaar. He loved to lose himself in its maze of streets, idling from one vendor to the next, sampling the fragrance of the perfumer; watching the potter throw the clay; admiring the deft touch of the enameller; savouring the touch of silk. To be in this city was to encounter, each day, a catalogue of wonders. Manus was shrewd enough to know that humans are no better or no worse from one place to the next. But Istanbul delighted him and, for the moment, that was enough.

Manus woke and dressed hours before the time appointed. He sat in the shade of the palace gardens, awaiting the Sultan's pleasure. There was a luxury in anticipating everything that was going to happen. He conjured up a picture of Beyazid robed in a splendid, black silk caftan. He saw the sunlight gleam on the golden threads of its embroidered flowers. He saw the airy, tiled room where the Sultan would greet him. He saw the carpets and cushions on the floor, the delicate porcelain bowls and jugs. He saw himself conversing with the Sultan. He imagined every moment of what was to come. The Sultan rising and inviting him to rise. The golden inkwell and pen held by the servant on the velvet cushion. The formal embrace and then the presentation of the gifts to mark the honour. It was like a dream come true. Brimming with joy, Manus surveyed his surroundings. Yes, he loved this corner of the palace garden. He loved the cool of the cypress trees, the damp trickle of water, the sound of the fountain and the rivulet flowing at his feet. He loved the bright flowers of the oleander bushes. Closing his eyes he enjoyed the warm, dry air. Here peace was to be found. He had travelled far from his home, but the voyage had led to this moment.

Footsteps approached. A servant, in white robes and turban, greeted Manus and invited him to follow. Manus thanked him. Calmly he rose to his feet, brushed back his hair and straightened his caftan. The moment had arrived. He thought of Saul. He thought of his dear father. He thought of Marie-Thérèse and Christoph. He knew they would all be proud of him. He tried the title: "Manus O'Rourke, Master of the Sultan Beyazid." He liked the sound. He smiled. Then Manus strode forward to meet his destiny.

Also published by Poolbeg

THE LONG MARCH

BY

MICHAEL MULLEN

After the Battle of Kinsale, on the last day of the year 1602, O'Sullivan Beare left Glengarriff in County Cork with one thousand of his followers, the remnants of a race defeated by the English in a cruel war. They set out to reach the safety of O'Rourke's castle in Leitrim. Two weeks later only thirty-five people reached their goal. The rest had perished on the way or abandoned the march.

This is the story of that march, a story of passion, suffering and heroism. It is the story of Emar and her brother Fiach who endured the bitter winter weather as harassed outlaws and had to face tragedy along the way.

Michael Mullen recreates one of the most remarkable episodes in Irish history in this gripping and stirring novel for young readers.

ISBN: 1-85371-890-4